THE ARSENIC MILKSHAKE

AND OTHER MYSTERIES SOLVED BY FORENSIC SCIENCE

SYLVIA BARRETT

Doubleday Canada Limited

Canadian Cataloguing in Publication Data
Barrett, Sylvia, 1950–
    The arsenic milkshake — and other mysteries solved by
forensic science

ISBN 0-385-25423-7

1. Murder – Canada – Investigation. 2. Forensic sciences –
Canada. I. Title.

HV6535.C3537 1994   364.1'523'0971   C94–931135–9

Jacket photograph by Ken Davies Photography
Jacket design by Tania Craan
Text design by David Montle
Printed and bound in the USA

Published in Canada by
Doubleday Canada Limited
105 Bond Street
Toronto, Ontario
M5B 1Y3

To Stephanie and Paul

ACKNOWLEDGEMENTS

To the dozens of forensic scientists and police officers who gave so generously of their time and expertise during the researching and writing of this book, I am deeply indebted.

I owe special thanks to Glenn Carroll of the RCMP's central forensic laboratory in Ottawa, now the force's intellectual property manager, for his tireless efforts in answering countless queries and for helping to ensure the book's technical accuracy.

For allowing me to spend days touring their busy laboratories and interviewing their staffs, I also thank Assistant Commissioner R. A. Bergman, former director of the RCMP Forensic Laboratory Services; Superintendent H. R. Williams, former director of the Ontario Provincial Police Technical Support Branch; and George Cimbura, Acting Director of the Ontario Centre of Forensic Sciences.

I am grateful to Bart Bastien and Chico Newell of the B. C. Coroners Service for their valuable insights and assistance in many areas of the book, and to journalists Noreen Flanagan of the *Daily Free Press* in Nanaimo, Judith Lavoie of the *Times-Colonist* in Victoria and Mary Lasovich, who kindly contributed background information on a little-publicized Vancouver Island murder trial covered in the chapter of forensic entomology.

At Doubleday, Jill Lambert, John Pearce and Maggie Reeves patiently guided the manuscript through its initial draft. Editor Shelley Tanaka deftly helped shape it into its final form.

I am grateful to the Canada Council for its support at a critical midway point, and to Chris who kept the lights on and the computer running throughout.

To my family and friends who lived with this book almost as much as I did over what sometimes seemed an interminable period of time, I owe my greatest debt. Carol Couillard helped organize intimidating mountains of material into relatively manageable files; Lib and Ralph Boston, Tom Burton, and Jan and Bob Reade offered idyllic retreats for intensive research and writing; David Lees and Neil Reynolds provided advice and encouragement; and so many others contributed in hundreds of different ways. I am especially grateful for the tremendous friendship and support of: Brenda Porteous, Peter Watson, Marilyn and Jim Davies, Sue Botting, Donna Jacobs, Carol MacKinnon, Valerie Voight, Pam and Jim Forsyth, Dorothy Maclean, Anne Kershaw, Jane Derby, Karen Lynch, Jill Greenaway, Ann Robinson, Sharon Kirkey, Richard Barnett, Michelle and Jack Broughton, and Anne and Jim Shepherd. My most heartfelt thanks go to my parents, Betty and Don Barrett.

CONTENTS

Introduction   ix

1   The Arsenic Milkshake   1

2   Crime Labs: From the Beginning   23

3   Making the Crime Scene Talk   51

4   Dental Sleuths   73

5   The Eloquent Dead   95

6   Bones   123

7   Maggots as Clocks   141

8   Biological Calling Cards   155

9   Science on the Stand   175

Index   204

INTRODUCTION

I N THE SPRING OF 1987, a
notice came across my desk at *Equinox* magazine, where I
was science editor, that the International Association of
Forensic Sciences was holding its eleventh meeting in
Vancouver that summer. The city was chosen not for its
magnificent natural setting or its cosmopolitan outlook but
because it was home to the association's president, James
Ferris, who was chief of forensic pathology for the province
of British Columbia.

It was only the second time that the association had
convened in Canada; it met in Toronto in 1969, when Doug

Lucas, director of the Ontario Centre of Forensic Sciences, was president.

In the intervening two decades, science had revolutionized the task of solving crimes with high-tech instruments and new methods of analyzing traditional evidence. The most dramatic of these developments had occurred only a few years earlier: a British geneticist had devised a way to distinguish everyone in the world, with the exception of identical twins, through a process called DNA profiling. Science writers around the world had jumped on the story, and awareness of the contribution that scientists have made to crime solving suddenly surged.

The program for the Vancouver meeting was not compelling reading. Even the most interesting symposia had titles that were either jargon-laden or soporific. But "Footwear and Tire Impressions" aside, I was more than a little intrigued.

A telephone call to Ferris cemented my interest. He described the unique team approach to homicide investigations that had evolved in British Columbia over the previous decade. To complement the expertise of specially trained police officers and scientists who work full time in forensic laboratories, the B. C. Coroners Service appointed not only a chief forensic pathologist but also a chief forensic dentist. And that was not all. On call from Simon Fraser University, the University of British Columbia and the B. C. Provincial Museum were botanists who could determine from disturbances to the vegetation when bodies had been buried; entomologists who could estimate from the insects feeding on decomposing remains when the victim had died; and a physical anthropologist to retrieve and identify skeletal remains.

These newcomers to homicide investigations, unlike

forensic pathologists, had "regular" jobs with no traditional connection to crime of any sort, much less murder. Yet within the quiet, sterile surroundings of their offices and laboratories, they regularly analyzed the gruesome artifacts associated with unnatural deaths. And, unlike the scientists who work in the country's major forensic laboratories and rarely go to crime scenes, the academics were increasingly joining the police and forensic pathologists on the front lines.

Shortly after that telephone call, I flew to B.C. to meet with these new scientific sleuths and some of their partners within the RCMP and its forensic laboratory. I found a remarkable group of people who generously shared with me their experiences and insights. Through their stories, and a couple of show-and-shock sessions looking at colour photographs and videotapes of murder scenes, I was quickly disabused of Hollywood's sanitized version of murder. By appreciating that it is a horrifying business with sights and smells so ugly they defy the imagination of the uninitiated, I found the contribution of everyone who spends time in it all the more inconceivable.

This book evolved from the *Equinox* article I subsequently wrote. It goes beyond the initial players to provide a behind-the-scenes look at a wider group of modern scientific sleuths in Canada. It does not purport to cover every aspect of forensic science, however, or even most of the country's forensic scientists, unsung heroes all, who toil away year after year in the country's major forensic laboratories making less money than they could in private enterprise, and regularly facing gruelling courtroom attacks on their credibility and their evidence — the hallmark of our adversarial legal system.

What it does is introduce a handful of these curious, dedicated individuals and some of the cases they have worked on, from the coroner who got his start cutting the grass at a funeral home at the age of eleven and recently had a retirement party in Vancouver's old city morgue with refreshments served on storage crypts, to the serious young female PhD student who became Canada's first full-time forensic entomologist and now earns her living, in part, picking maggots out of decomposing corpses. Through their stories, I hope readers will appreciate that Canadian forensic scientists take a back seat to no one. They may not be as well known as their counterparts in the FBI and the British Home Office, but they are right up there at the cutting edge of each and every forensic frontier.

THE ARSENIC MILKSHAKE

N ORM ERICKSON never met Esther Castellani. He was a young chemist breaking into the field of forensic biology in Toronto when she was mysteriously dying in a Vancouver hospital. But, almost thirty years later, he can still recall the exact date of her death: July 11, 1965. And he is still awestruck at how close her killer came to getting away with murder.

Esther was born in Calgary in 1925, one of three children of Swiss immigrant Karl Lound and his British wife, Mabel. The family moved to Vancouver when Esther was still a child, and at age fifteen, after completing grade eight, she left school to work as a bakery helper. Six years later, at Holy Rosary

Cathedral, she married René Castellani, a charming Montreal-born general contractor who, like Esther, was of European parentage, twenty-one and Catholic. In 1953, the couple had a daughter.

By 1964, Esther was working as a sales clerk in a children's clothing store on West 41st Avenue, and René was a well-known on-air personality in the promotions department at radio station CKNW in New Westminster. He had the gregarious nature of a successful publicity agent; she was a pleasant, plump woman who enjoyed a simple life centred around the family's tiny duplex at 2092 West 42nd Avenue. Her employer and neighbours knew her as a responsible worker who was devoted to her family, and happy.

In August, Esther and her daughter accompanied Esther's parents on a three-week motor holiday to San Francisco. She was disappointed that business pressures had prevented her husband from joining them but, in typical fashion, was cheerful throughout the vacation.

Several weeks after their return, Esther and her mother were at the Hadassah Bazaar when Esther complained that she had been feeling intermittently nauseated. Her mother was not worried; she attributed it to the trip, to "too much riding" in the car.

Esther was not particularly concerned either, even by New Year's, when she was also experiencing abdominal pain, dizziness and a strange sensation in her hands. She did, however, consult a general practitioner whose office was across the street from her workplace. She admitted to the doctor that she liked to eat and was not as careful as she might be with her diet. When his examination revealed nothing abnormal, he determined that she had a simple case of gastritis, or inflammation of the stomach; he cautioned her about her nutritional habits and gave her medication to ease the nausea.

The doctor heard nothing more until the middle of March, when Esther's husband telephoned him late one evening to report that his wife was in acute distress with abdominal pain and vomiting. He examined her again that night in her home and came to the same conclusion. After giving her an injection to quell the nausea, he lectured her more sternly about the importance of a good diet.

At the end of March, the Castellanis moved to a duplex with a garden at 2509 West 41st Avenue; on two follow-up visits with the doctor, Esther reported that she was feeling much better.

In May, however, the doctor received two more late-night calls from Esther's husband, asking if he could come immediately to their home. On one occasion, she had become violently ill after eating bacon; on another, after consuming a hamburger with mushrooms. After the third house call, the physician placed her on a standard ulcer diet. Over the next week, her condition seemed to improve. When her symptoms returned on May 21, he arranged for her to undergo a gallbladder x-ray.

Although Esther was still not depressed or anxious about her condition, her mother was growing increasingly concerned. She told her son-in-law she thought they should get a second medical opinion and, with his consent, she called on Bernard Moscovich, a specialist in internal medicine at Vancouver General Hospital.

When Moscovich examined Esther in her home on May 23, the only abnormality he found was a slight tenderness across her upper abdomen. He suggested that she follow the advice of her family physician unless her symptoms became worse; in that event, she should consider going into hospital for further investigation.

The next evening, Esther's condition was much worse. Her husband and mother drove her to the emergency department at Vancouver General Hospital, where she was admitted. In addition to a tender abdomen, she had a flushed face, elevated pulse and low blood pressure. She was in good spirits, though, her mother later said, because "like everyone else, she thought she was going in there to get better."

In the face of intensive medical testing and care, Esther's health continued to see-saw. For the first three weeks, her hands and feet remained numb and painful, but the nausea and vomiting disappeared. Apart from one eight-day period when he was involved in a publicity stunt for his radio station, René was frequently by her side, as were her mother and other family members. Their visits helped her maintain a relatively positive attitude.

On May 28, for example, the nurses' notes on her chart state that she had spent a comfortable afternoon and good evening with no complaints. On June 3, she was still slightly unsteady on her feet but, for the first time, spent short periods sitting up in a chair. On June 11, she said there seemed to be a slight decrease in the numbness in her hands; the next day, she had her hair done.

Inexplicably, though, on June 13, shortly after eating dinner, she again began vomiting intermittently; a few days later, she told the nurses that she felt as if she had tourniquets on her hands and feet.

4
◆

Moscovich was stumped. The only irregularity revealed in myriad laboratory tests and x-rays was a low white blood cell count, possibly indicating a reaction to a toxic agent. After intensive questioning, Esther remembered that she had helped with some spray-painting at the store early that year; however, a subsequent test for lead poisoning came back negative.

During the last half of June, Esther's condition had rapidly deteriorated. Her arms and legs were so weak that she could not stand up, feed herself or even hold a cigarette. The tingling sensations, which had spread to her knees and neck, now felt like hot needles. Her skin was covered with tiny blisters, and she had severe diarrhea. She spent long periods crying.

With René's permission, Moscovich called in specialists in haematology, neurology and physical medicine. The consensus was that Esther was suffering from an acute viral infection from which she would probably fully recover. By the beginning of July, however, she began to show early signs of heart failure. The burning in her neck and knees had escalated to the point that ice packs were needed to control the pain. And her already poor appetite diminished further. Moscovich ordered blood transfusions and sent samples of her urine and blood to the provincial health laboratory to confirm that she was, in fact, suffering from a virus.

On the morning of July 9, the nurses' notes state that her breathing was shallow and rapid; she was coughing up mucus and she needed constant ice bags for the severe burning pain in her feet. They put an oxygen tent over her bed and changed her position frequently; still, she was unable to get comfortable, became anxious and agitated, and refused all food and fluids.

At two-thirty that afternoon, Moscovich placed her on the seriously-ill list and notified her husband of her grave condition.

The next day, in spite of the oxygen tent and medication, a lack of oxygen in Esther's blood caused by her increased heart failure turned her lips and fingernails blue. The cyanosis was worse the next morning. At 10 a.m., her respiration was extremely laboured, but she was conscious and moaning. At 10:17 a.m., with her husband by her side, her breathing stopped. A priest performed the last rites, and Moscovich pronounced her dead.

Moscovich would not receive the negative results of the virus testing for another two weeks, but his gut already told him something quite different was wrong. Immediately after Esther's death, he gently asked René Castellani for permission to have a clinical autopsy performed, to study the disease process. Later the same day, after talking it over with his sister-in-law and a close friend, René returned to the hospital and signed the necessary papers.

On July 12, a routine post-mortem was conducted. Moscovich watched as pathologist Frank Anderson first inspected the exterior of the body and then meticulously removed each internal organ, examined it inside and out, weighed it and cut off a small sample and placed it in a bottle containing the preservative formaldehyde. Anderson found that the lungs were twice as heavy as normal and filled with red blood cells, which is consistent with heart failure: when the heart becomes so damaged that it cannot pump blood out, the blood backs up into the lungs, causing death. Overall, however, the lungs and heart appeared normal, as did the other organs. In short, Anderson could find no reason for Esther's heart to have failed. With the medical mystery still unsolved, he took additional samples of the heart and liver to be frozen in case further studies were needed.

Moscovich was unhappy. The autopsy had merely confirmed what he already knew: Esther had died of heart failure. But why? He left the morgue determined to find out. At home that evening, he spent several hours poring over Esther's medical history. By rewriting and summarizing all the findings and observations during her seven-week stay in hospital, from the nurses' notes to the copious test results, he confirmed that whatever the cause of her illness, it had affected her gastrointestinal tract, nervous system, blood, kidneys and heart. He then listed every possible cause of such a gross insult to the body.

Hospital tests had already excluded such conditions as diabetes. And after analyzing the data, Moscovich was able to rule out rare types of neurological and connective tissue diseases. The only possibility left was that Esther had been suffering from the effects of some type of toxin, as her initial blood tests had indicated. He knew from the tests that it wasn't lead. Slowly and methodically, by comparing the symptoms of other chemical substances to her history, he discounted all but one. To his utter dismay, he realized that Esther could have died of arsenic poisoning.

Moscovich had attended forensic medicine lectures covering the subject and, some years previously, he had treated miners who had accidentally inhaled arsine gas. He knew there is no clear-cut reaction to the ingestion or inhalation of arsenic, but in every case the whole body is affected. The more he thought about it, the more convinced he became.

The following day, he shared his suspicions with Frank Anderson.

On July 14, Esther's body was buried in a casket, inside a cement crypt, at Forest Lawn Memorial Park in Burnaby. A week later, tissues preserved at the autopsy were sent to the City Analyst's Laboratory for toxicology testing; the lab was specifically asked to look for traces of arsenic.

The initial analysis was primitive. Chemist Alexander Beaton took slices of the heart, liver and kidney, which had been fixed in formaldehyde, and subjected the mixed sample to what is known as Gutzeit's test. Simply put, this burns off the organic matter and converts any metallic arsenic present into arsine gas; when exposed to a strip of paper soaked in mercuric bromide, the gas leaves a quantifiable yellowish-brown stain.

Minute traces of arsenic are normal in the human body; in the heart, liver and kidneys, for example, levels usually range from 0.024 and 0.039 parts per million. In his first experiment, Beaton found 24 ppm — 1,000 times the expected amount. He repeated the test and got an even higher reading. Before sounding the alarm, though, he analyzed the formaldehyde in which the tissues had been preserved, as it was possible that the fluid had somehow become contaminated. When he determined that it had not, he notified the head of the toxicology laboratory, Eldon Rideout. Since the investigation had turned from a purely medical one to a potentially criminal one, the coroner's service and the police then took over.

On August 3, Esther's body was exhumed and taken to the coroner's morgue. The same morning, in keeping with the procedure of first investigating immediate family, detectives with the Vancouver City Police homicide squad paid a visit to René Castellani at his home on West 41st Avenue. He was co-operative, and raised no objection to accompanying them to the police station for questioning. And, on their return, he readily gave them permission to search his house. The officers confiscated more than two dozen items they found in the kitchen and bathroom — everything from dental powder and cough syrup to baking soda and cream of wheat.

Back in the morgue, as forensic pathologist Thomas Harmon conducted the second post-mortem on the body, he had an advantage not afforded Anderson at the original autopsy: he knew where to look. In general, when arsenic is ingested, it is absorbed from the bowel into the bloodstream and from there, in varying concentrations, into the organs. The liver, for example, whose job it is to eliminate the toxin, takes up more than the brain. It is the nerve tissues, though, that tell how the person died. When death is caused by a single lethal dose of arsenic, there is damage to the brain and spinal cord, but not to the peripheral nerves. The situation is reversed when small doses of the poison are ingested over a long period.

After carefully examining the coffin to ensure that nothing could have seeped in after burial, Harmon extracted samples of peripheral nerve tissue and examined them under a microscope. He found that the insulating sheaths surrounding the nerves had virtually disappeared and the nerves themselves were damaged to varying degrees. It explained Esther's numbness and burning sensation, and it proved that she had been poisoned slowly. But over how long? For that information, Harmon turned to the hair.

Within an hour of arsenic entering the body, hair roots begin to soak up the chemical the way blotting paper does ink. Arsenic does not wash out; each dose is permanently recorded by every growing strand of hair on the body. From several areas of the head, Harmon took clumps of hair and placed each in a plastic bag.

In his laboratory, Rideout took the hairs and sectioned them into one-centimetre pieces, which he analyzed separately using Fisher's method, which is similar to Gutzeit's but five to ten times more sensitive. The results revealed that Esther had been ingesting arsenic for at least seven months: hair grows about one centimetre a month and there were abnormally high levels of the poison in the seven centimetres of hair nearest the scalp.

More telling, though, was that the highest concentration was in the hair closest to the head. That meant she had taken the largest doses while she was in the hospital. Since she was unable to feed herself then, it ruled out the remote possibility of suicide. Someone had to have given it to her.

Over a three-month period, Rideout examined a total of 300 separate items, from the tissue samples to the household products taken from the Castellanis' house. He discovered that the fingernails and skin taken from the exhumed body contained up to 110 times the normal levels of arsenic. The heart tissue taken at the original autopsy contained 800 times the standard amount; the liver tissue, 1,500 times. The body could not have been contaminated after death because there was no arsenic in the embalming fluid. And even if the coffin had not been tightly sealed, there were only trace amounts in the soil in which it had been buried.

While Rideout was compiling the physical evidence, the police were looking for a motive for the crime. They discovered that René Castellani was not the loyal husband that his telephone calls to the doctor and his visits to his wife in hospital had suggested. In fact, since the summer of 1964 when Esther and her daughter were vacationing with her parents in California, René had been having an affair with a twenty-five-year-old receptionist who worked at the same radio station.

Neighbours of the woman, who was known by her friends as Lolly, said the two had talked about getting married months before Esther died; René said he was in the process of getting a divorce. Twelve days before Esther's death, René and Lolly had gone together to look at a small three-bedroom bungalow that was for sale; he told the builder and a real-estate agent that they were getting married in two weeks and had planned a holiday together in Disneyland.

Two days after the funeral, the couple set out on the trip with René's daughter and Lolly's young son. René had told everyone that he and his daughter were going away alone, but then booked into the Kona Kai Motel in Anaheim, California, which was owned by relatives of a co-worker at CKNW. He introduced Lolly as his sister-in-law. That fall, they moved with their two children into a house at 6331 Argyle Street.

The pieces of the puzzle seemed to be falling into place when Rideout showed that a can of weed-killer taken from Castellani's kitchen cupboard, from which three ounces were missing, was 53 percent sodium arsenate. The detectives had questioned René when they found it alongside household cleaners and a shoe-polishing kit. He said he hadn't seen it before. On second thought, he said he thought it was lighter fluid for the barbecue.

As suspicious as it seemed, however, the facts meant nothing on their own. Many husbands had affairs, René's fingerprints were not found on the can of herbicide. And the Castellanis' house, to which they had moved in April of that year, had a backyard garden. At an inquest ordered by the coroner's service, the jury ruled that Esther had died "at the hands of a person or persons unknown."

A year earlier, the case might have been relegated to an unsolved-murder file. However, 1965 marked a juncture in Canadian forensic toxicology. Researchers had discovered that they could use a sensitive new radio-chemical technique called neutron activation analysis on hair to date the ingestion of poison. The Ontario Centre of Forensic Sciences in Toronto had just acquired the only equipment in the country capable of conducting the tests, and Norm Erickson, a biologist at the centre, was already using the instrumentation for hair analysis.

Erickson had joined the Ontario lab in 1959 after obtaining a bachelor's degree in chemistry at Queen's University in Kingston. He had planned to go into teaching but says he got sidetracked when his mother mailed him an interesting story on forensic science she had cut out of *Reader's Digest*. After reading the article, he went to talk to the Ontario Provincial Police and was directed to the attorney-general's department, which ran the Ontario lab.

A tall, lean man with short, curly hair and glasses, Erickson says his love of nature has kept him going over the past thirty-five years in the biology section, first as a junior analyst and eventually as department head. Over the years he has worked on some macabre cases, including the case of the wig that turned out to be a human scalp. The murderer had fashioned a hairpiece out of his victim's scalp to disguise himself as a woman when he crossed the border into Canada from New York State. "You see some horrific things," he says, "and they come back, you think about them. What really upsets me are the ones involving children. But I try to get out and paddle my canoe once in a while. You know, get out and walk around and look at all the beautiful things."

Looking back to the Castellani case, Erickson says, "I have worked on some interesting cases, but that is one of the biggest that ever came down the pike for me."

In the early 1960s, after nearly two years of training in serology and hair and fibres at the Ontario lab, he was sent to the University of Toronto for another two years to work on the research and development of various applications of neutron activation analysis. One of the initial goals was to use the technique to match a single hair found at a crime scene to a specific person on the basis of its elemental composition. But it turned out that too many of us have the same elements present in our hair and that individual hairs from the same person can give different readings. The procedure was also time-consuming and costly. In the case of Esther Castellani, however, neutron activation analysis proved to be worth its weight in gold.

Eldon Rideout's experiments had provided a rough time frame for the poisoning. Hoping that Erickson could provide much more specific evidence, Rideout sent him by registered mail samples of complete hairs, including the roots, which he had taken from the exhumed body. It was the first time in

Canada that neutron activation analysis would be used to track the ingestion of poison in a murder case.

In principle the test was simple: the hair was irradiated in a nuclear reactor to make any arsenic radioactive. Then the gamma rays it gave off were measured on a scintillation counter. In practice, it was painstaking. Erickson worked long hours on the case that fall, going into his laboratory on weekends to expedite the project. One by one, he took the hairs, placed them under a stereo binocular microscope against a fixed ruler and cut them with a scalpel at a precise point. He sliced a first batch into one-centimetre lengths, each of which represented a one-month period. A second batch was sliced into half-centimetre lengths, each signifying two weeks. A last batch was cut quarter-centimetres, each depicting a week. Using tweezers, he then transferred each tiny fragment to a polyethylene capsule that contained the identical part from the other hairs in that lot. By irradiating each container individually, he could determine how much arsenic was absorbed during each time frame.

Since the nuclear reactor at the University of Toronto was not powerful enough for this type of testing, every time he had to irradiate some containers, Erickson had to drive almost an hour from his lab in downtown Toronto to Hamilton to use the reactor at McMaster University. He well remembers the wary looks of other motorists as he drove back in his '61 Chevy, his lead-encased cargo in the trunk and red-and-yellow radiation warning signs on his car windows. He made six of these trips for the Castellani case.

Erickson's diligence paid off. When scientists in Vancouver collated his fine-tuned findings on a chart, the irregular peaks and valleys corresponded to Esther's acute bouts of vomiting and her subsequent recoveries. Consistent with her medical history, the graph showed that the doses became greater and greater until, in the last week before she died, her hair absorbed 768 ppm of arsenic. The normal content is 1 to 3 ppm.

With strong evidence that arsenic was administered every time Esther was sick, the investigators began comparing the dates on which she took violently ill with other events. They made an interesting discovery.

At the beginning of June, while Esther was in the hospital, René Castellani was involved in a publicity stunt for a car dealership on Broadway. Called "Guy in the Sky," it required him to live for a week in a station wagon perched on a pole twelve metres off the ground. During that time, he did live broadcasts around the clock on the success of the sales campaign. While the promotion was going on, Esther felt much better. On July 13, the day after it ended, she became violently ill again.

Armed with the link they needed, the police combed the hospital, interviewing every member of the staff who had cared for Esther. One nurse recalled that René had asked her to tell Esther's mother to leave one evening when visiting hours were over, rather than staying late as she usually did, so that he could visit with his wife alone. Two others said they saw René take milkshakes into his wife's room on several occasions, although they did not see the empty containers after he left.

On a similar note, Esther's sister-in-law, Sheila, remembered an odd incident that occurred on July 6, a week before Esther died. She had walked into Esther's room and found René trying to force her to eat a homemade dinner of ground beef and string beans, which her mother had brought to the hospital the previous evening in an attempt to perk up her daughter's appetite. When Sheila saw that Esther was becoming increasingly distressed by René's insistence, she told him to put the food away. René replied, "She's got to eat, she should eat." Eventually, Sheila reached across the bed and took the bowl of food from René's hands. He responded, "If she is not going to eat, why don't you throw it into the toilet." Sheila ignored him and began adjusting Esther's pillows. He kept insisting that she dispose of the food until, finally, she did. When she asked him why that was necessary, he said that Esther's mother would be happy if she thought her daughter had eaten the meal. Shortly afterwards, a nurse came into the room and, seeing the empty bowl, commented to Esther, "Oh, good girl. You have eaten all your dinner." René answered, "Yes, pretty good, eh?"

During the same visit, Sheila told investigators, she asked René in the hallway outside Esther's room whether the doctors had determined yet what was causing her illness. He answered, "When a house is burned down I don't look for what started the fire, I look for how you build a new one."

On another occasion, a nurse's aide said she had met René in Esther's room late one evening at the end of June. Her shift was ending and he offered to drive her home. During the eight-minute ride, René asked her point-blank when she thought Esther was going to die. He explained that he had bought his wife a new appliance and he did not know whether to pick it up from the store.

As the police broadened their investigation, they learned that René had been attributing his wife's illness to a toxin long before there was any medical or scientific evidence of the cause. And his stories were inconsistent. He told a couple of people that Esther was suffering from lead poisoning as a result of painting she had done. He told others that she had become sick after either using weed-killer on her own garden or inhaling herbicide that had been sprayed on a neighbour's yard. "It's just a matter of time," he told one acquaintance in early June.

If René had been lacing Esther's food with weed-killer, though, wouldn't she have known? Back in his laboratory, Rideout mixed tiny amounts of the solution into ground beef and milkshakes. Like pure arsenic, the herbicide was tasteless, odourless and did not curdle.

On March 31, 1966, less than nine months after Esther's death, René and Lolly applied for a marriage licence. At midnight on April 6, René was arrested at their home on Argyle Street and charged with first-degree murder. He opted to be tried by a jury.

The public lined up to get into the trial, and the courtroom was packed. In addition to the large crowd of spectators, including several prominent members of the legal profession from both sides of the border, there were forty-six Crown witnesses.

Norm Erickson was on the stand for two and a half days, during which he was examined, cross-examined, re-examined and re-cross-examined seven times. "It was gruelling," he recalls. "I was a little apprehensive. You are always apprehensive when you go to court. You never get over that. But a highlight for me was that Melvin Belli, the famous criminal lawyer from San Francisco, who happened to be in the city at the time, was present when I was giving evidence."

The defence counsel, A. A. Mackoff, aggressively challenged Erickson's dating of the arsenic ingestion, citing conflicting figures on the growth rate of hair from one particular textbook. Erickson explained that he had conducted his own research on how fast female human hair grows, and his findings agreed with those reported by other scientists who had conducted similar trials.

"Have you written any texts on this subject?" Mackoff asked him.

"No, sir," Erickson replied. Maintaining his composure, the young biologist continued to resist Mackoff's attempts to get him to change his opinion.

Mackoff also attempted to erode the credibility of Bernard Moscovich, the physician who attended Esther in hospital. How could he be qualified to testify as an expert on the subject of arsenic, the defence lawyer argued, when he had failed to diagnose arsenic poisoning in Esther before she died?

The Crown's strongest witness was Harold Taylor, head of the departments of pathology at the University of British Columbia's medical school and Vancouver General Hospital, who interpreted and summarized the medical and scientific evidence for the all-male jury. On the basis of Erickson's experiments, Taylor told the court, "In my mind, there is no question at all that this individual has received or absorbed arsenic in multiple doses over a period of at least five months."

Taylor added that Erickson's findings explained the clinical picture reported by Moscovich: the development of neuritis and then paralysis, the kidney changes, the anaemia and, finally, Esther's death from heart failure.

In his cross-examination, Mackoff suggested to Taylor that the same type of neuritis was compatible with a lack of vitamins, diabetes or a virus of unknown origin. "That's correct," the doctor replied. Mackoff then noted that the negative results from the virus test conducted on Esther did not rule out the possibility that she was suffering from a virus that researchers were unable to classify. "Or one they didn't look for," Taylor said. He added that as a physician, pathologist and scientist, knowing the clinical history, the autopsy findings and the results of the laboratory analyses, "I still have to come back to my own considered opinion that she did, indeed, die of chronic arsenic poisoning."

Mackoff questioned Taylor about how much arsenic was found in Esther's body and how this compared with the minimum lethal dose. The total amount of poison could not be calculated, Taylor said, but the laboratory results showed that her liver alone contained half a grain, or one-quarter the minimum amount known to have killed someone.

"Now, Dr. Taylor, the amount of arsenic required to be ingested to cause death varies from person to person, is that not so?" Mackoff asked.

"Yes, I think so," said Taylor.

"And this would be the case in both acute and chronic cases."

"Yes."

"Now . . . there are people with these readings or higher readings who could have lived?"

"I can't honestly answer that because I don't know of . . . any person who has lived in which one can examine the heart, liver, kidneys and so on."

In his final address to the jury, Mackoff argued that the

Crown's case was purely circumstantial. If René had been a "diabolically clever" murderer, why didn't he dispose of the can of weed-killer or hide the milkshakes he took to his wife in hospital? And why did he give permission for an autopsy to be performed? "A guilty mind would have asked for the cremation of the remains."

Mackoff added that the person who administered the arsenic to Esther had to have known how much to use and what to mix it with: "I say to you it must have been done with an almost scientific exactness and precision because, otherwise, one little bit too much and there is a sudden death. . . . There is not one tittle of evidence . . . that the accused has any such knowledge or that it was within his competence to administer it with that exactness."

In his charge to the jury, the judge noted that "a man may lead a double life or may behave in a most peculiar manner, but that doesn't say he is a criminal. . . . As defence counsel says, there are many cases of liaisons in this city and every other city, and merely because a person is not getting along with his wife and established a second home is no conclusion that he is going to get rid of his wife in the most direct way by killing her."

The judge also agreed with Mackoff that the case was circumstantial. However, he told the jury not to be afraid of that: "Circumstantial evidence is, many times, the only evidence that is ever produced in a trial . . . where a crime is committed by stealth or by secrecy [and] there aren't eye witnesses. . . . It is not necessarily less reliable than direct evidence. In fact, often it is more reliable because a conclusion based on circumstantial evidence, you see, doesn't rest upon one single fact, upon one witness who may be lying or who may be unreliable. It rests upon . . . in this case, a great body of facts or a great body of circumstantial items, if you like, that are not facts until you accept them, of course."

The jury deliberated for four hours. It found René Castellani guilty of capital murder and recommended no clemency. Minutes later, Mr. Justice J. C. Ruttan sentenced Castellani to death by hanging.

In 1967, the British Columbia Court of Appeal ordered a new trial in the case. Although the judges ruled that the evidence had conclusively proved that Esther was murdered in a planned and deliberate manner by arsenic poisoning, they questioned the trial judge's remarks to the jury regarding Castellani's character. "While evidence of [his] untruthfulness and deceitfulness and of his relationship with the other woman was properly admissible in proof of motive, the charge could be construed as an invitation to the jury to consider . . . that he was the kind of person who would be likely to commit the crime."

At his second trial, in 1969, Castellani was again found guilty. By this time, the death penalty was no longer in effect in Canada. In May 1979, thirteen years after his initial arrest, he was paroled from B.C.'s Matsqui Prison, where he had been well liked by the other inmates and had attracted a large number of women visitors. On his release he moved to Nanaimo and remarried. He eventually admitted to acquaintances that he had killed his wife, but he told a convincing tale of her dying of terminal cancer, and portrayed his actions as merciful euthanasia. Ironically, he died of cancer five years later.

For his part, Norm Erickson still wonders what would have happened if Bernard Moscovich had not been quite so uneasy about the diagnosis of acute viral infection; if, simultaneously, the Ontario lab had not just received the first equipment in the country capable of neutron activation analysis . . .

The now greying scientist shakes his head. It's a coincidence like this, he says, that has helped sustain his belief in a higher power.

CRIME LABS: FROM THE BEGINNING

A**FTER IT WAS CONVERTED** into an odourless, tasteless powder by an eighth-century Arab chemist, arsenic became such a popular murder weapon that it was dubbed the "inheritance powder." It is somehow fitting that the development in the mid-1800s of the first apparatus to detect minute traces of the metallic poison in its victims would herald seventy years of momentous discoveries in forensic science and, ultimately, the establishment in 1910 of the world's first laboratory devoted to these disciplines.

For more than a thousand years, countless individuals who stood in the way of others' ambitions endured agonizing deaths after unwittingly ingesting the readily available poison. Even kings and nobles, who had tasters, were not immune. Because the victims' symptoms, including diarrhea, vomiting and stomach pains, mimicked those of cholera, which was widespread in the Middle Ages and after, only the most blatant of poisoners were apprehended. The rest went free because the substance was impossible to trace in the body. In 1836 that changed.

A penniless British chemist by the name of James Marsh designed a simple device that provided visual proof of arsenic's presence. A predecessor had already discovered that when either sulphuric or hydrochloric acid is mixed with any fluid containing arsenic and then exposed to zinc, arsine gas is produced. Marsh fashioned a U-shaped glass tube with one end open and the other tapered and fitted with a nozzle. He attached a piece of zinc to the nozzle and poured fluid with arsenic and acid into the open end. When the liquid reached the zinc, arsine seeped out of the spout. He found that if he ignited the gas as it escaped, and held the flame against a piece of cold white porcelain, even the tiniest amount of arsenic produced a black deposit.

Four years after Marsh's discovery, a Spanish doctor used the apparatus to convict twenty-four-year-old Marie Lafarge of killing her husband, Charles, in France. And, in the process, the science of toxicology was introduced to the world. René Castellani used almost the same method to murder his wife more than a century later. Ironically, he, too, was brought to justice by a new scientific technique and suffered virtually the same fate as the young French woman.

Marie was an aspiring aristocrat; Charles, a failed industrialist with peasant roots. Introduced through a marriage broker, Marie thought her dreams had come true when Charles wooed her with stories of wealth and a country estate. When, too late, she discovered he had lied, she was devastated. She waited until her new groom went to Paris on a business trip and sent him a passionate love letter and an arsenic-laced Christmas cake. He fell ill after eating just one piece, but survived and returned home weak and unsuspecting.

Continuing to feign affection, Marie pampered her husband with truffles and other treats that she had sprinkled with arsenic. As Charles's condition deteriorated, his family called in two doctors; both diagnosed cholera and one suggested he be fed eggnog as a "strengthener." Eleven days after his return home, he was dead.

Marie might have gone free, except that a member of the Lafarge household had seen her stir white powder from a small pill box into a glass of eggnog and had locked away the beverage after Charles took a few sips. She turned the liquid over to the local gendarmes, who also gained possession of the pill box. When the police learned from an apothecary that Marie had purchased a large quantity of arsenic, ostensibly to kill rats, just before she mailed the cake to her husband and, again, before he returned home, she was charged with murder.

After a few botched attempts by local chemists to analyze the exhibits, the prosecutor at her trial called in Mathieu Orfila, a doctor widely regarded at the time as Europe's expert on poisons. Using Marsh's device, Orfila found arsenic not only in the eggnog and the pill box but in Lafarge's stomach and other organs. Marie was sentenced to life in prison. She was released after ten years with tuberculosis and died a few months later.

News of the trial — and a fierce debate on the validity of Marsh's test — circled the world. The technique stood the test of time, however, and helped pave the way for chemists and doctors — usually pathologists — to become the first formally recognized forensic scientists. In 1859, a Canadian pioneer in the field of toxicology, Henry Crofts, a professor at the University of Toronto, was asked to examine the body of an Ontario woman believed to have been poisoned by her husband. The German-trained chemist testified in April of that year that he had found five times the minimal lethal dose of arsenic in the stomach of Sarah King. Dr. William Henry King of Cobourg was subsequently convicted of murder and executed.

The King trial is believed to be one of the first times that medical evidence was introduced into a court in Ontario. Forensic science, which is any science applied to legal issues, was not organized in North America or Europe, however, for another half a century. In the interim, there was a series of discoveries that still form the cornerstone of modern identification techniques. But before they were accepted as fact, they were subjected to considerable scepticism and, in some cases, downright ridicule.

In 1877, a British civil servant reported a new method of confirming identity that was far superior to photography. Over the previous nineteen years, William Herschel had taken thousands of fingerprint impressions and had determined that no two prints are alike. Furthermore, he found that fingerprints do not change over time: an individual's prints are the same at death as they were at birth. Herschel made the discovery while working in India, where he had sought to differentiate among superannuated soldiers, many of whom could not write and some of whom he suspected were collecting several pensions. Although Herschel's findings were independently verified by a Scottish physician working in Japan, a full three decades later the pre-eminent French forensic pathologist Edmond Locard was pushed to burn his own fingers in a series of painful experiments to prove the unadulterability of fingerprints. Even then, in 1912 an American court refused to accept the principle.

Whereas Herschel's revelation met with disbelief, the efforts of Alphonse Bertillon, the father of the study of physical measurements, which he called anthropometry, were greeted with outright mockery. In 1879, while a file clerk with the Paris Prefecture of Police, Bertillon twice wrote to the prefect about a method of identifying and classifying criminals that he believed to be far superior to the vague written descriptions and fuzzy photographs that the police had been collecting in an attempt to identify habitual criminals. His system was based on the fact that the length of an adult's bones remains constant, and the chances of two people having the exact same sizes on eleven specific body measurements — including overall height, length of arms, fingers and feet, and length and circumference of head — are slightly higher than four million to one.

Bertillon informed his superior that he had begun organizing the precinct's files of criminals according to rough groupings of these measurements and, in future, would be able to quickly determine whether an arrested person had previously been charged.

Eventually, he was granted an audience with the prefect who, unable to understand the mathematics of probability, had conferred with his chief detective; he promptly dismissed the theory. Expecting accolades, Bertillon instead received a stern warning: stop bothering us with your hare-brained ideas or you'll be fired. Buoyed, however, by subsequent encouragement from his father, a distinguished physician and statistician, Bertillon refused to abandon his system. Four long years later, to the surprise of all present, he gleefully produced a file card that proved a suspect had been apprehended a year earlier on theft charges and had changed his name.

The young clerk finally won formal approval for his experiments, but his colleagues continued to laugh at him. The derision stopped the following year, when he identified no fewer than three hundred previous convicts. The year after that, his system was introduced in every prison in France, and Paris newspapers lauded him for his ingenious method. In 1888, Bertillon was named director of the police identification service and was assured a prominent place in history, even after fingerprinting, a simpler and more accurate method of identification, overtook Bertillonage.

In 1900, an assistant professor at Vienna University made an even more important discovery, one that would form the basis of modern serology. Experimenting on his own blood and that of his colleagues, Karl Landsteiner determined that human blood can be divided into four main types — A, B, AB and O. To say the importance of this breakthrough was not immediately appreciated is an understatement. It was not until thirty years later, when he was working at New York's Rockefeller Institute, that Landsteiner received the Nobel Prize for his work.

By the turn of the century, Sir Arthur Conan Doyle had been writing his Sherlock Holmes stories for two decades, yet the value of science to the detective stayed within the realm of

fiction until 1907, when a landmark book advocating the application of advancements in science and technology to solving
crime was translated into English under the title *Criminal
Investigation*. It was written by Hans Gross, a professor of criminal law at the University of Graz, Austria, who had spent two
decades learning about chemistry, physics, microscopy, botany
and zoology. Three years later, the University of Lyons'
Edmond Locard became the ultimate advocate of forensic science when he established the world's first laboratory devoted to
analyzing the physical evidence in crimes.

Following in Locard's footsteps, forensic pathologist
Wilfrid Derôme, who had studied forensic medicine in Paris
for two years, opened North America's first forensic laboratory, in Montreal in 1914. Established under the auspices of
the Quebec attorney-general, it remained the only forensic
lab on the continent for nearly two decades. In 1932, following two visits to Montreal, J. Edgar Hoover set up the FBI's
crime lab in Washington, D.C. And the Ontario Attorney-
General's Department established a medico-legal laboratory
— later the Ontario Centre of Forensic Sciences — at 11
Queen's Park Crescent in Toronto. It had a staff of two —
pathologist Edgar R. Frankish and chemist Verda Vincent.

The RCMP got into the act in 1937, opening its one-
man forensic laboratory in Regina. That man was Maurice
Powers, a young surgeon from Rockland, Ontario, who had
studied forensic medicine at McGill University under
Rosario Fontaine, Wilfrid Derome's successor and a former
student of the great Locard in Lyons.

Powers had written to the commissioner of the RCMP
on June 24, 1936, asking for the job after hearing that the
force was conferring with the FBI and Scotland Yard about

setting up a "scientific crime detection laboratory" to serve the force and other federal government agencies. The recent graduate had spent eighteen months as an intern at Montreal General Hospital before accepting a position as resident physician at Royal Ottawa Sanatorium. But his real interest, as he had stated in the McGill yearbook, was "murders."

The fact that his father was the local coroner in Rockland and would have been well known to many police officers may have given Powers an edge over other candidates. Even though it was scientists and others outside of police departments who had made the most remarkable contributions to forensic science over the past century, there was still a widely held belief among the police that solving crime was best left to them. In the early thirties, Lucas S. May, president of the Northwest Association of Sheriffs and Police, summed up this feeling in a letter to the RCMP commissioner.

> Doctors and chemists, ordinarily without a criminal investigation background, are unsuited to this class of work. The ideal examiner of physical evidence, of course, is a man who primarily has an investigation background, who is above all a successful detective and investigator and then who has the technical knowledge and skill to make such examinations as are submitted to him. . . . So many things will occur to the experienced investigator which would not occur to the doctor or chemist, who have not been trained along investigative lines, that any comparison between the two types are odious.

Conflicting opinions about the roles of scientists in criminal investigations would continue to rage in the forensic community for decades. Nonetheless, on December 30, 1936, Powers was signed on as a special constable to the force at a starting salary of $1,800 a year, a modest sum even in those days and $250 less than an RCMP inspector earned. He was promptly shipped to the Office of the Chief Medical Examiner of New York City for seven months of practical instruction in forensic pathology. In August he was appointed Surgeon to the Force, and his annual salary was bumped up to $2,250.

In a memo dated August 10 and introducing the young doctor to the head of the Regina Depot, the site of the force's training camp, the commissioner of the RCMP noted:

> As Surgeon Powers has had no training, will you please have an officer give him such personal instruction, particularly in saluting, as is necessary for a surgeon in this force. As soon as a course of instruction in the Constable's Manual and Criminal Code is commenced for a recruits class, Dr. Powers is to attend all such lectures during normal recruit training, likewise any lectures on these subjects by Inspector Jones or others to advanced classes.
>
> The equipment for the laboratory is now being purchased and the question of accommodation will depend on the transfer of the present kitchen and mess room to "B" block. Surgeon Powers has submitted his plan for the accommodation required for the laboratory which is provisional, making use of the present kitchen and basement as well as half of the present mess room. This will leave you half of the present mess room to be used as a lecture room.
>
> Until such time as the laboratory is ready to operate, Dr. Powers, while not employed in giving lectures is to be detailed to "F" Division as much as possible to accompany members of a busy detachment, such as the Town Station on investigations and accidents in order that he may gain police experience.

By the late thirties, the RCMP was policing the Prairie and Maritime provinces, as well as the Northwest Territories. The memo ended with the instruction that Powers visit as many divisions and subdivisions in the neighbouring provinces as possible.

Initially working out of a single room above the officers' mess, Powers assembled a small team of uniformed officers, including the legendary "Robbie" Robinson, whose treks around the northern tip of Great Slave Lake during his first posting to Fort Reliance in the Northwest Territories helped earn him a place of honour in the force's history. Patrolling the region on dog sled, the young Mountie regularly spent weeks at a time in the frozen wasteland. On one such trek in the winter of 1935, he was away for twenty-five days and travelled 1,145 kilometres. When the dog food he had packed for his huskies ran low, he hunted caribou to feed them.

Chronicles of his many feats also mention a gentle side: when a raw recruit turned up at the Regina laboratory one day with a button missing from his sleeve, Robinson told him he was improperly dressed and asked him to take off his jacket. As the trembling novitiate looked on, the seasoned officer reached into his desk drawer, took out a needle and thread and sewed on a button from his own stock.

Powers chose Robinson to become the force's first authority on hair and fibre identification. Three other Mounties were recruited to study and specialize in the other "police sciences" of the day. Stephen Lett was assigned to "questioned documents," John Mallow to fingerprints and photography, and James Churchman to ballistics.

The team was inundated with requests for its services even before it moved its first microscope into its freshly decorated laboratory in May 1938. During the last five months of 1937, they scrutinized 1,245 exhibits, printed more than a thousand photographs, gave 467 hours of lectures and spent sixty-two days testifying in court.

As quickly as the demand for these services sprang up, it became apparent that it was impractical to ship exhibits from eastern Canada to Saskatchewan. Consequently, in 1942, the force set up a second lab, in Ottawa. For the next fifteen years, these two facilities handled all of the work coming to the RCMP from its own police forces and from provincial and municipal police forces, federal and provincial government departments, and members of the legal community in areas not served by the Ontario and Quebec labs.

Tragically, Powers died in an airplane crash in 1943 after he and two RAF members collided with a string of telegraph poles while attempting to follow the railway tracks from North Battleford to Saskatoon through a blinding snowstorm at night.

In the early days, the directors of all of Canada's forensic laboratories often travelled great distances to testify in court. On the opening day of the fall assizes in 1951, for example, H. Ward Smith, a pharmacologist and newly appointed director of the Ontario laboratory, had fourteen subpoenas to answer from Sault Ste. Marie to Cornwall. He managed to attend all but one of the courts by cutting back and forth across the province in police cars. Although the laboratory had by then relocated to more spacious quarters in the old Hospital for Sick Children on College Street, and was handling more than five hundred cases a year, it employed only two staff in addition to Smith:

pathologist Noble Sharpe and a technician.

In the fifties, the demand for the services of Canada's forensic laboratories set a breakneck pace that continues unabated today. By 1957, the Ontario lab — then bursting at the seams with seventeen staff and eighteen hundred cases a year — was forced to move again, this time into an 11,000-square-foot space in an inartistic but modern two-storey building at 8 Jarvis Street.

The same year, the RCMP opened its third lab, in Sackville, New Brunswick. Unlike the Ontario and Quebec labs, which operate independently of any police force and have always been staffed strictly by civilians, the RCMP initially had a policy of hiring only police officers to staff its laboratories. The two notable exceptions were Powers and Frances McGill, a pathologist who, after retiring from the Saskatchewan Attorney-General's Department, was recruited after Powers's death to help John Mallow run the lab for a couple of years. In 1946, in recognition of the service she had provided, McGill was appointed honorary surgeon to the force — the first and only woman to hold such an appointment.

To keep up with the demand for laboratory personnel, the force instituted a program through which designated officers were sent to university, at public expense, to obtain the academic qualifications required by their new posts. Only when the growth in forensic science surpassed the rate at which such education could be provided was a policy of employing university graduates as civilian members of the labs instituted. By 1969, half of the technical staff working at the RCMP forensic laboratories were civilians; twenty years later, more than 80 percent were.

Although there has never been a shortage of young men and women eager to embark on careers in forensic science, there has traditionally been insufficient money to properly recompense them. Before the Ontario government opened its medico-legal lab in Toronto in 1932, for example, its forensic autopsies were handled by a small group of surgeons at the old Grace Hospital in the city. In 1923, when Noble Sharpe was hired by the hospital as its pathologist, he was asked if he would also do the backup laboratory work for forensic autopsies. He agreed. Six months later, he submitted a bill to the Attorney-General's Department for the extra work. He was informed that there was no money to pay him. "Since the surgeons were only paid $15 an hour," he wrote years later, "no payment could be expected from them." He added, perhaps naively, "Although it had not been intended that way, the principle on which forensic pathologists continued to work for a considerable period of time, i.e., out of a sense of civic duty, was thus initiated."

Even after the first labs were established, and in spite of the widespread acceptance of forensic science in Canada and around the world, the budgetary constraints continued. The RCMP's Sackville laboratory, for example, was first set up in unused space in a federal Department of Agriculture building on the Mount Allison University campus. The makeshift accommodations had several less than desirable features, which were pointed out by Insp. Andrew Mason-Rooke to his superiors: "We find ourselves exceedingly cramped and unable to install some necessary equipment. . . . The bullet recovery apparatus is housed separately in a chicken shed a quarter of a mile away and also, due to lack of space, we are unable to install photographic facilities sufficient to employ a photographer, but are forced to send negatives for enlargement and processing to the Ottawa laboratory for court illustration purposes."

The opening of the RCMP's fourth lab, in Vancouver in 1963, was seen partly as a cost-saving measure. Three years earlier, a federal member of Parliament had suggested in the House of Commons that it would be cheaper to open a new facility in British Columbia than to continue to fly scientists from the Regina lab to the West Coast. About that time, a civilian serologist with the Saskatchewan lab logged 142,500 kilometres in one year for court appearances.

During the 1970s, the RCMP opened four new labs, in Edmonton, Winnipeg, Halifax and Montreal. Their establishment coincided with the introduction of a wave of high-tech instruments with revolutionary applications for crime solving: scanning electron microscopes that could magnify particles hundreds of thousands of times, allowing the viewer to analyze airborne fluff one micrometre — one millionth of a metre — in size; mass spectrometers and gas chromatographs that could separate complex compounds — from drugs to fire residue — into their individual components and identify them; and computers that could mix and match megabytes of information within seconds.

At the forefront of this technological revolution, discoveries in nuclear science were first applied to the field of toxicology. As a direct result, neutron activation analysis was introduced, and René Castellani was convicted of murdering his wife. Soon after, scientists at the Ontario centre resolved a century-old case of suspected arsenic poisoning using the same radiochemical technique.

In the 1860s, an American explorer, Charles Francis

Hall, set out on an expedition to the North Pole. When winter came earlier than expected, he and his team were forced to set up camp in Greenland, where Hall subsequently died, apparently of natural causes. A hundred years later, his biographer, Chauncey Loomis, became convinced that Hall had been murdered and obtained permission to exhume the body from its burial site in the permafrost. Samples of the explorer's hair and fingernails were sent to Toronto, where analysis confirmed Loomis's suspicions: Hall had ingested large doses of arsenic.

In 1973, the Ontario lab was asked to investigate another hundred-year-old case because of lingering doubts that justice was served. This was none other than the assassination of Thomas D'Arcy McGee. At two in the morning on April 7, 1868, the Irish expatriate walked the short distance home from the House of Commons where, as one of Sir John A. Macdonald's cabinet ministers, he had just finished delivering an impassioned speech against a motion to dissolve Confederation. As he unlocked the door to his boarding house at 71 Sparks Street, a shot rang out, and he fell dead on the sidewalk. The prime minister and the police were immediately summoned and carried the body into the house, where another boarder, Dr. Donald McGillvray, performed an autopsy in the attic. McGillvray determined that McGee had been killed by a single bullet that had entered the back of his neck, exited through the upper lip, driving out four artificial teeth, and hit the door.

The following day, acting on a tip, Det. Edward O'Neill of the Ottawa police department arrested Patrick James Whelan, a red-haired tailor's assistant who was active in Irish societies and had been in the public gallery during

McGee's last speech. When apprehended, Whelan had a fully loaded revolver and a box of cartridges in his pocket, which in itself was not uncommon at that time. The evidence against Whelan at his trial was mainly circumstantial, apart from the testimony of some dubious witnesses. The jury heard, among other things, that a piece of tailor's burlap, with the initials P. E. on it, was found in an empty house across the street from McGee's boarding house; Whelan worked for tailor Peter Eagleson. It also heard that Whelan had campaigned for McGee's opponent in the election of 1867 and had called McGee a traitor, who if elected would never be allowed to serve. Other witnesses testified that they had heard Whelan admit the shooting to prisoners at the jail.

The trial lasted seven days and was attended on two of those by the prime minister and his wife. Whelan was found guilty. In February, he was hanged outside the Nicholas Street jail in front of five thousand spectators, at what was the last public execution in Canada.

Questions about Whelan's guilt were still being raised in 1970 when Timothy Slattery, a Montreal lawyer and author of a book on the assassination, contacted the Ontario Centre of Forensic Sciences after learning that, although the gun was long gone, the fatal bullet still existed in the Archives of Ontario. Slattery asked then director Doug Lucas if the type of revolver that had fired the bullet could be identified. Lucas said he thought so, and soon after, the historic artifact arrived at the lab inside a tiny metal box with the letters J. A. MCD inexplicably scratched on the bottom. Remembering that the prime minister had sat beside the judge for part of the trial, Lucas concluded that the court clerk was looking for a suitable container for the exhibit and was handed the box by Macdonald.

Although the bullet was badly oxidized, the centre's firearms experts determined from their examination and a literature search that it had been fired from a Smith and Wesson .32-calibre revolver. Among the thousands of confiscated firearms in its "weapons library," the centre had a similar pistol. The analysts were able to show that bullets fired from it were consistent with the McGee bullet and reported their findings to Slattery. It turned out that Whelan had been carrying a Smith and Wesson when he was arrested. However, the centre also learned that fifty of these guns, made in January or February of 1866 and sold by J. W. Starrs of New York for $13, were shipped to a Montreal dealer that year.

McGee was assassinated two decades before the 1889 discovery that forms the basis of firearms identification. That year, Alexandre Lacassagne of Lyons, a pioneer of forensic medicine, who had already established that the time of death can be estimated from the extent of lividity, or blood settling, in a corpse, first suggested that a gun barrel leaves distinctive marks on bullets. Scientists later discovered that, in fact, every barrel leaves a unique mark, a sort of ballistic fingerprint, on the bullets it fires. Knowing this, and using a comparison microscope, they could see whether a crime bullet matched a test bullet fired from a suspected murder weapon into a water tank or a cotton-filled box. But at the time Whelan was tried, no one knew of a way to link his revolver to the bullet that killed McGee.

Three years after the centre examined the bullet, the gun that killed McGee turned up. It seems O'Neill, the police officer who had investigated the murder, had kept it as a souvenir after the trial and eventually passed it on to his nephew, who in turn gave it to a younger friend. When the latest owner read Slattery's book and realized the significance of the weapon, he gave it to Mary Burns, a historian with the National Capital Commission in Ottawa. She turned it over to Lucas after, he says, the RCMP seemed interested only in whether it was registered.

Just as the centre's firearms experts had said, the weapon was a Smith and Wesson .32-calibre six-shot revolver. When they cleaned and oiled the gun, it fired normally into a test block of Plasticine mounted on a slab of wood. The recovered bullet bore a remarkable resemblance to the one that killed McGee. Justice, it seems, had been served after all.

Today, the five hundred or so scientists and technicians working in Canada's major forensic laboratories struggle to keep up with exhibits from current crimes. Budgetary constraints forced the RCMP to close its Sackville and Montreal labs in the early 1990s; the staff at its six remaining labs handle about seventeen thousand cases a year, which in 1992 included 572 murders. In Quebec, Direction des Expertises Judiciares takes on seven thousand cases a year, including about two hundred homicides. And the country's largest lab, the Ontario Centre of Forensic Sciences, now occupying the first eight floors of a modern highrise near the provincial legislature, and its small satellite lab in Sault Ste. Marie handle about 8,500 cases, of which two-hundred-odd are murders.

In 1992, the RCMP spent $24.7 million on operation and maintenance of its six labs and another $2.6 million on equipment. The total budget for the Ontario Centre of

Forensic Sciences in 1993/94 was $11.2 million. Although all forensic labs provide their services free of charge to their "clients," they impose priorities on services. In 1992, the federal government asked the RCMP — which must balance the need for more microscopes against the need for additional police cars — to look into the feasibility of user fees for non-RCMP police forces who use their laboratories. The "spirited reaction" of police clients caused the plan to be dropped, noted Dr. H. W. Peel, director of forensic laboratory services. "One ancillary benefit of the exercise," he added, "was the improved appreciation of the economics of laboratory operations."

The labs are divided into half a dozen sections: biology, firearms, toxicology, chemistry, photography and documents. The RCMP has a separate section for alcohol analyses and also operates a central bureau for counterfeits. Analysts in every section face a certain amount of plain old-fashioned drudgery — they call it grunt work — in the course of their jobs.

Staff in toxicology, for example, spend the bulk of their time on impaired-driving cases, using mass spectrometers that can detect one billionth of a gram of any one of five hundred drugs in bodily fluids and tissues. Chemists armed with high-powered microscopes, gas chromatographs and infrared spectrometers scan countless tiny chips of paint to determine the make, model and year of manufacture of vehicles involved in hit-and-run accidents. Handwriting experts in the documents section, assisted by microscopes, computerized video systems and electrostatic detection equipment, examine innumerable forged cheques, bogus lottery tickets and stolen credit card vouchers. Staff in photography use enlarged pictures, infrared lights and micro-scopes to determine whether the paper match came from this exact book, the sandwich bag used to hold drugs from this roll. Even in the biology and firearms sections, which are involved in murder investigations more often than the other departments, staff peer through microscopes at seem-ingly endless hair, semen and blood samples or, in the firearms section, at screwdrivers and other tools used in incalculable break-ins.

Referring to the repetition, an analyst at the RCMP's central lab wryly comments, "I don't know if I have eighteen years of experience, or one year's experience repeated eigh-teen times."

Although their everyday cases don't make headlines, the scientists who work in the country's forensic labs are not com-plaining; they enjoy their jobs to the point that they settle for salaries far below what they could earn in private industry. They are a naturally curious bunch whose dedication some-times leads them to experiments that surpass the bounds of duty. Just as Edmond Locard once burned his own fingertips to prove the unadulterability of individual prints, Doug Lucas of the Ontario centre recalls one experiment that he and some of his staff conducted during one of the most famous and, ultimately, controversial trials in Canadian history.

Steven Truscott was a fourteen-year-old resident of Clinton, Ontario, who was convicted of raping and murder-ing his classmate Lynne Harper on June 9, 1959. He told the police that he was riding his bicycle around seven that evening when Lynne asked him for a lift to the highway. He agreed; after dropping her off, he saw her get into a new grey Chevrolet. Witnesses confirmed that Steven was with

Lynne after supper, but said he was alone by 8 p.m.

The Crown's case centred around the time of death. The regional pathologist who performed the autopsy estimated from the time the victim ate dinner and the subsequent contents of her stomach that she was killed two to two and a half hours after she ate, or between 7:15 and 7:45.

The Ontario centre was not involved directly in determining the time of death, an issue that was hotly contested at the trial and for years afterwards, and was ultimately a factor in Truscott being released from prison after ten years. However, Lucas and his colleagues were asked to determine whether the stomach contents proved that Harper's last meal had, in fact, been the turkey and peas she ate with her parents around 5:15 that evening. They found it was. To do so, Lucas, Norm Erickson and a handful of others ate a duplicate meal and, at varying times afterwards, put their fingers down their throats and regurgitated. An analyst then compared their stomach contents with the victim's.

Such experiments are not the stuff of day-to-day routine, but most scientists can recount a few cases that stand above the rest — real mysteries that make up for the days spent painstakingly straightening out a ball of tightly crumpled aluminum foil so that it doesn't rip, for example, or feeding information on the frequency of a particular subclass of acrylic fibre, or the density and refractile index of a sample of glass, into their computer databases to improve the significance that can be attached to future findings.

For Michael Philp, assistant head of the biology section at the Ontario centre, one of those special cases began late on a Friday afternoon in 1978, when he received an excited telephone call from Finn Nielsen. Nielsen is the Danish-born head of the centre's firearms section who spends his holidays rubbing shoulders with such Hollywood stars as Geena Davis and Burt Reynolds while he oversees firearms safety precautions on movie sets and corrects directors' misconceptions about what happens when a person is shot.

"Come up and take look at this," Nielsen told him. "I think there are some fibres attached to this bullet."

That's impossible, Philp thought to himself. The bullet had been surgically removed from a member of the Satan's Choice, one of several bikers charged with the murder of a rival biker at a Port Hope, Ontario, bar. During the fracas, according to eye witnesses, three bullets were fired; the police initially recovered only two. When Gary Comeau was arrested, he told police that he had been sitting to the right of the victim when a man suddenly appeared at the victim's left and shot him point-blank several times. As the deceased slumped to his right, Comeau said he felt something hit him high in his left arm — the spot from which the third bullet was eventually retrieved.

On his way up to the sixth floor to examine the recovered bullet, Philp was sure Nielsen was mistaken; he must have seen some strings of muscle tissue. When he peered through the microscope, he was incredulous. "I really did a double take when I saw them. You could tell right away that they were fibres. Five or six of them had embedded themselves in the soft lead. Then it was a question of identifying them."

Philp gently wrapped the bullet in Kleenex, gingerly placed it in a little plastic box and carried it, chalice-like, back to his fourth-floor lab. The analyst worked until eight that evening, first identifying the minuscule threads under a low-powered stereo microscope and then comparing them by size, colour and composition with the constituent fibres of the victim's shirt. Sure enough, they all matched, corroborating Comeau's statement that he was sitting to the right of the victim when the shooter appeared on the left. Apparently, one of the bullets grazed the victim before hitting Comeau. Philp immediately called Comeau's lawyer to report his findings; the following Monday, he gave his evidence in court.

Although physical evidence is generally considered more reliable than eye-witness accounts, in this case, for reasons known only to them, the jury members decided that the scientist's testimony was not sufficient to discount the word of two Crown witnesses who said they saw the wounded biker fire three shots into the victim's head. Comeau was convicted of first-degree murder and sent to prison for life.

Five other bikers were convicted as accomplices in the case, even after a seventh Satan's Choice member, who was never charged, told the jury that he shot the victim in self-defence. His testimony was apparently disregarded because he had a previous conviction for perjury.

The real story may never be uncovered, yet the fibre evidence would seem to support Comeau's unwavering assertion of innocence. In the spring of 1994, after he had spent fifteen years behind bars and all normal appeals had been exhausted, he was granted permission by a judicial review jury, under a special section of the Criminal Code, to apply for full parole.

Fibres also played a crucial role in one of the biggest cases for Barry Gaudette, a widely respected expert in hair and fibre evidence.

During a twenty-two-month period beginning in July 1979, some thirty boys and young men went missing in

Atlanta, Georgia. Fibrous debris removed from the bodies of twelve of those found dead suggested their murders were linked.

Eight bodies were retrieved from rivers in the area. The first of these was clothed. However, after an Atlanta newspaper reported that scientists at the Georgia Crime Laboratory had recovered fibres from victims, the last seven were naked or nearly naked when they were pulled out of the water. Even so, the scientists were able to find fibres and foreign hairs on all of them.

Police and FBI agents staked out the Jackson Parkway Bridge, which crosses the Chattahoochee River in northwest Atlanta. At 2 a.m. on May 22, 1981, after the surveillance team heard a loud splash, they apprehended Wayne Williams as he drove slowly off the bridge. Two days later, his last victim, twenty-eight-year-old Nathaniel Cater, turned up one and a half kilometres downstream. Williams was charged with murdering Cater and Jimmy Payne, twenty-one, whose body had been pulled out of the same river.

Cater's body was discovered completely unclothed; Payne's wore only shorts. Nonetheless, FBI analysts recovered animal hair and five types of fibres from the victims' hair and the one piece of clothing. They determined that three of the fibres and the animal hair were common to both bodies, and one or more of the hair and fibre samples matched finds on the corpses of ten other murdered boys and young men in the area.

Gaudette, who was then head of the hair and fibre section of the RCMP's central lab in Ottawa (and is now head of biology), was asked by the FBI to assess the significance of their evidence against Williams and to testify at his trial.

This was not unusual. Canada's major forensic laboratories share expertise not only with one another but also with such American and European agencies as the FBI and the British Home Office. And the RCMP labs had been examining hair and fibres since the mid-1930s when Robbie Robinson was recruited as the force's first authority in the field.

By 1981, the FBI had routinely done hair and fibre examinations and comparisons for more than thirty years — and, like their Canadian counterparts, could work with threads a mere five millimetres long. Still, there was extensive pretrial scepticism in Atlanta about the value of fibre evidence, even within the law enforcement community. While it had often been used to corroborate testimony in a homicide case, it had not, until then, been the key evidence in any case involving multiple murders. Newspapers and magazines, hungry for leads in the sensational case, ran numerous articles outlining the microscopical procedures used in the characterization and comparison of textile fibres and speculating on the significance that would be attached to the findings.

To assist the Fulton County, Georgia, Supreme Court jury in understanding the evidence, FBI analysts prepared more than forty charts and 350 photographs, in which the fibres were magnified up to six hundred times.

Gaudette confirmed their findings: the fibres were all consistent with fabrics in Williams's home and cars, including a yellowish-green nylon rug and a violet acetate bedspread in his bedroom, as was the animal hair with the family's German shepherd. Furthermore, none of the fibres was common. The carpet, for example, was manufactured only in 1971 and in small quantities. Gaudette concluded that it was virtually impossible for any environment other than the suspect's house and cars to have produced the combination of hair and fibres found on the victims. On February 26, 1982, the jury found Wayne Bertram Williams guilty of two charges of murder.

Another American was convicted of murder as a result of old-fashioned sleuthing by the Ontario Provincial Police combined with sophisticated analyses by scientists in the biology, toxicology and chemistry sections at the Ontario Centre of Forensic Sciences.

Kimberly Jean Woodward of Saginaw, Michigan, went missing on February 18, 1980. She was last seen being chased from her apartment by her ex-husband, Gene; when she had not returned home the next day, her sister called the police. A month later, a farmer and his son were walking through a snowy woodlot off Highway 21, near Goderich, Ontario, when they saw what they thought was a badly burned calf lying in the hollow created by an upturned tree. They telephoned the Ontario Provincial Police who, on closer examination, determined that the remains were human. Careful excavation of the area turned up fifty-six associated exhibits, including various pieces of fabric, grey duct tape, plastic and several sections of rope.

An autopsy revealed that the victim was a woman, between the ages of twenty and twenty-five, with a slender build and light brown hair. She had suffered a blow to the back of the head, and had a ligature mark on her neck, suggesting that she had been strangled. The report added that the extreme charring of the entire body indicated that an accelerant had been used in the fire.

It was not much information to go on. In fact, the case

might never have been solved if the killer had not overlooked a crucial piece of evidence. In the ashes under the woman's left hand, the police recovered charred engagement and wedding rings. Cleaned by a local jeweller, they offered the first breakthrough in the case. Beneath the carbon, now clearly visible, was a trademark, Magic Glo.

The detectives traced the name to an American company, which gave them another piece of good news. They had shipped only twenty-eight identical ring sets to five retailers in the United States. Since the closest outlet was in Saginaw, the police started there. Leroy's jewellery store had sold five sets, it said, and could provide the names of all buyers. The police found the first four owners alive and well. The fifth customer was Gene Woodward.

When the police came calling on April 14, Woodward nervously blurted out that the officers must be there about his missing ex-wife. The next day, he set off with his son and second wife, telling neighbours he planned to start a new life in Texas.

When dental records positively identified Kimberly as the murdered woman, the police returned to Gene's now abandoned home. After retrieving some rope from a box at the side of the driveway, they began tracking him down. When they caught up with him in Texas, they confiscated his 1971 Opal, from which they recovered hundreds of fibres from the trunk.

In the meantime, scientists in three sections of the Ontario lab were starting to get results. Chemist Louisa Newbury had determined from analyzing the vapours from the burnt debris and soil collected at the scene that gasoline had been used to fuel the fire. Toxicologist Frank McAuley learned — from the lack of carbon monoxide and the traces

of ethyl alcohol he found in samples of the victim's blood —
that she was not alive when she was set afire and, in fact, she
had been dead for some time because her body was decomposing. By June, Newbury had also discovered that grey duct
tape removed from the victim's face was indistinguishable
from tape found at the suspect's home. Finally, by late fall,
biology head Norm Erickson had found that a piece of green
12-ply rope found around the body was similar in construc-
tion and colour to that removed from the driveway, and that
numerous fibres taken from the trunk of the Opal matched
the multicoloured afghan wrapped around the body, pieces
of which remained unburned on the underside.

A police check on Woodward's licence plates clinched
the case. By fluke, a constable on routine patrol had stopped
Woodward's car just after midnight on March 23, some
eighty kilometres from where the body was found.
Woodward had been driving back towards the border. The
officer noted at the time that he seemed nervous and that the
woman with him was crying. After the jury in a Michigan
court heard the evidence from the Canadian scientists and
detectives, Woodward was convicted of second-degree murder and sentenced to life in prison.

Woodward never did confess; he was found guilty solely
on the basis of the physical evidence. As juries demand more
and more of this type of evidence for convictions, the job of
the police technicians who collect it has become increasingly
important. And just as the scientists working in Canada's
forensic labs have sophisticated new methods and high-tech
equipment for analyzing the exhibits, so, too, do today's
identification officers at the scene.

MAKING THE
CRIME SCENE
TALK

BRIAN STRONGMAN remembers it as the case of the twice-buried body. At the end of May 1986, in a secluded forest west of Ladysmith, on Vancouver Island, a hydro surveyor was checking out a swath that had been clear-cut for power lines. At the edge of the woods, he came across what appeared to be a human bone. Strongman was head of the identification section at the RCMP's Coquitlam detachment when the call came in.

"Ident" officers are the front-line troops in crime-scene investigations. Their job is to find the physical evidence that will identify the perpetrator — everything from fingerprints and tool marks to hair and fibres — and then photograph, videotape and, sometimes, sketch the scene. To do that, they require considerable experience as police officers and increasingly specialized training: the RCMP currently has a handful of ident specialists with expertise in interpreting bloodstain patterns or recovering buried remains. As important as their formal qualifications, though, is their capacity to be patient, attentive to detail and utterly analytical.

Two hours after the surveyor's discovery, Strongman arrived at the scene by helicopter; an identification officer with the nearby Nanaimo detachment and two other Mounties — a homicide investigator and a general duty officer — were waiting. Strongman, who was called in because of his expertise in buried remains, identified the bone as a human pelvis. From the dirt clinging to it, he knew it had been buried.

The foursome ventured into the heavy bush to search for the grave. Within a fifty-metre radius, they came across a stump that had been torn apart, probably by a bear looking for grubs, and pieces of vertebrae, some of them fractured and chewed by an animal. Then a scrap of blue jeans with the Lee label still attached, as well as a boot with a sock inside and, within it, toe bones. And, finally, a femur and more bits of blue jeans. But no grave.

"We couldn't figure it out," says Strongman. Normally, he would have suggested that they search for disruptions in the soil vegetation. In this case, though, the only clear area they came across was covered by a fallen tree, giving the impression that the ground there had not recently been disturbed, so they didn't check it. But they didn't give up, either.

After sizing up what they had uncovered so far, Strongman determined that the shreds of blue jeans were flowing in one direction; he got down on his hands and knees and crawled along the ground in the same line. Gradually, under the low-lying evergreen bushes spread over the forest floor, he found, like macabre trail markers, larger and larger chunks of fabric. Finally, beside the downed tree, he tugged on one that was partially buried.

The roots were intact, as if the tree had been naturally uprooted, and the sand all around it was smooth, as though it had been untouched for years. When Strongman lifted up the trunk, however, the soil underneath was lumpy. He knew he had found the grave. Indeed, several hours of careful excavation revealed the decomposed body of a thin young man with long dark hair and a missing front tooth.

Later, as he was examining the exposed remains in the shallow grave, Strongman noticed something odd. Although the bones of one leg were aligned with the remaining boot, two were transposed. The chain of events became clearer.

"What must have happened," he says, "was this guy was killed in the autumn. The perpetrator buried him hastily, not far below the surface. In the springtime, a bear came out of hibernation, got a whiff and dug him up, scattering pieces around, and taking what he wanted to eat to the edge of the clear-cut, where he could see what was going on while he chewed on the bones.

"The culprit then came back to look at the scene. Realizing what had happened, he gathered up everything he could find and reburied it, lining up the boot and everything — although I don't know why he went to that length. Then he took the log and laid it on top so the bear wouldn't dig it up again."

Strongman recalls with a chuckle that while he and the other officers were on their knees, painstakingly uncovering the body with masonry trowels and paintbrushes, they heard loud noises nearby: "It was funny. Here were all these big, hairy Mounted policemen bent over these rather smelly remains, and all of a sudden we hear this crashing through the bush. Someone said, 'The damn bear is coming back. Does anyone have a gun?' Not one of us did. It didn't come too close, though. There must have been too many of us."

There was another twist to the case of the body that was buried twice. The victim's skull was recovered in several pieces. When Strongman and a forensic pathologist examined these later at the morgue, they found two circular holes characteristic of a single bullet going straight through the head. The glitch was that the perforations were about fifteen millimetres in diameter — too large for anything short of, say, a 50-calibre machine-gun on an American battleship or, maybe, an old flint-lock rifle. And when the skull was pieced back together, the holes were slightly tear-shaped rather than perfectly round.

After talking with the RCMP's firearms experts, Strongman ruled out the possibility that the victim had been shot in the head. What, then, had created the holes? For weeks, he mulled it over, checking out every unusual murder weapon he came across. Finally, he hit on it. It must have been the circular end of a single-bar-style tire iron — the part used to remove nuts from wheel bolts. After searching out various makes and models, he discovered one with the perfect diameter. But there was still a problem: the end of the tire iron was definitely round, not tear-shaped.

"This thing was really bugging me," he says. Determined to figure it out, he conducted some rudimentary experiments. Out of Plasticine he fashioned several spheres the size of a head. Then he swung the tire iron at each ball from a different angle. *Voilà*. Straight on, the tool formed perfect circles with no crest. But angled just a little, the iron made holes that were a perfect match for the punctures in the skull.

If there is a modern-day equivalent to Sherlock Holmes, it is probably the identification officer. "Ident men are a strange breed," says Strongman, "a certain type of individual who thrives on analytical work. Not to the point that they want to stay in the crime lab all day. They like to be out working at the actual scene."

Individuals who are willing and able to work within the gruesome arena of homicide scenes often pay a price — and none more than identification officers. In the RCMP, for example, these 290 crime-scene specialists, of which about half a dozen are women, are the only police officers required to undergo annual psychological assessments. The experience of one veteran identification officer explains why. After a decade of working, day in and day out, with murder, he says he had a couple of clues that it was time to go into another line of police work. At one multiple homicide, in which an entire family had been killed, he found himself nonchalantly stepping over the mother's body on his way to the bathroom. Emotionally detached from his surroundings, he was thinking about what he had to pick up at the hardware store the next day. It wasn't until he looked into the mirror and saw the slain woman's reflection that the horror of what had happened hit him. About the same time, he found that every time he met someone new, he automatically pictured how they would look dead.

What keeps most of them going is the ability to view their work as a scientific exercise.

Operating on the premise that every contact leaves a trace — a principle articulated more than seventy years ago by Edmond Locard — the officers search for everything from a single hair or drop of blood to the tiniest fibre. As science has increased the ability to detect and analyze the most minute piece of evidence, the officers want to ensure that they leave no traces of their own. At most murder scenes, they now wear latex surgical gloves and disposable white hooded coveralls, which they call bunny suits.

Their appearance as characters out of a science-fiction movie is reinforced by the high-tech lights and tweezers they carry as they literally crawl over every inch of the scene. Until they have finished scouring an area, the other police and civilian members of the team, from the homicide detectives to the coroner, are not allowed into it. At complex scenes, a general duty police officer may be designated to document, package and distribute the exhibits; otherwise, the ident team does it. Most of the evidence they collect is turned over to scientists in the forensic labs. The task of processing and comparing fingerprints, footprints, tire marks and tool marks usually falls to the ident officer who collected them.

Eventually, the cornerstone of identification will be DNA profiling, but until then fingerprints remain the best way to identify someone. And, as natural problem solvers, identification officers are always on the lookout for new ways to uncover this traditional evidence.

In 1880, three years after William Herschel discovered that a person's identity could be confirmed by fingerprints, Henry Faulds, a Scottish physician working in Tokyo, reported in *Nature* magazine that he had assisted the Japanese police in catching two thieves by studying the prints left by their dirty fingers. Clean, sweaty hands might also leave impressions, he wrote, and the police should be on the lookout for these at all crime scenes.

Today, the police routinely lift prints that are not visible to the naked eye. But the means of accomplishing that task have recently burgeoned. In fact, there have been so many improvements over the past twenty years in illuminating latent prints that identification officers are now faced with choosing which process, or sequence of processes, is likely to be the most effective on the surface being examined. Some techniques work on the fats in sweat, for example; others with the salt or the amino acids.

Until the mid-1970s, crime-scene exhibits were either dusted with a powder or treated with a chemical. Not only does dusting inhibit some chemical methods but certain chemicals preclude one another. Ninhydrin, for example, which binds to the amino acids in perspiration, cannot be used after silver nitrate, which reacts with the salt, because the silver nitrate washes away the amino acids.

"The job is tricky because it is not divided into good and bad in terms of what you use," says Brian Dalrymple, a civilian identification technician with the Ontario Provincial Police. "You can't walk down both sides of the road. You don't know what would have happened if you had chosen a different technique."

Dalrymple graduated from the Ontario College of Art in 1970, intending to pursue a career in advertising. He soon decided, though, that he hated the intense pressure to be constantly creative. After short stints pumping gas and driving an auto parts truck, he applied to the OPP. While Dalrymple looks more like a TV cop than an artist, he had no intention of becoming a police officer; he was "just looking for a better job."

For the first year, he worked shifts — answering telephone queries from patrol officers about stolen property and outstanding arrest warrants. When a job came open in the forensic identification section of the OPP laboratory, where his visual training and photographic skills could be put to use, he jumped at it. At the OPP, civilian analysts work on fingerprint development, classification and comparison — a job normally done only by police ident officers; however, like their counterparts who work full-time in Canada's other forensic laboratories, they rarely attend crime scenes. Dalrymple spent his early days in the lab training and working under supervision on simple cases like recovering usable fingerprints from the fingers of victims of, for example, fire or drowning.

One of his first cases involved a man who went missing after he drove a truckload of chicken guts up to a giant hopper at a fertilizer plant. When a belt buckle and a fingertip were found in the mash, police surmised that he had somehow fallen down the chute. Dalrymple's task was to obtain a print from the digit; he did, but the man's identity could not be verified because no matching prints could be confirmed as his.

It would seem a gruesome job, particularly for someone with an arts background, yet Dalrymple says the work did not bother him: "I had been a hunter and fisherman for years, so I know what things are made of." In fact, looking back now as a senior forensic analyst in the section, he says he had found his niche.

Five years after he joined the OPP, Dalrymple was married and living in a duplex in Mississauga, working in the police lab and, like forensic biologist Norm Erickson, canoeing "anywhere there aren't many people" during his off hours. Then he embarked on a case that would ultimately open a brand-new door in fingerprint detection. He was trying an uncommonly used technique, known as iodine-silver plate, to lift prints from a piece of cheap cardboard. Our fingers don't secrete oil, but they do pick it up when we touch our faces. Iodine fumes adhere to the oil and, when a silver plate is then pressed onto the print, the fumes chemically react with the silver to form an image that can be photographed.

It was not working this time. Try as he would, Dalrymple could not get the iodine to transfer onto the silver plate. Mulling over the problem, he began to wonder if he could somehow induce the iodine to fluoresce and photograph the print directly, eliminating the need for the silver plate. He asked his friend and next-door neighbour Jim Duff, a chemist at Xerox. Their discussion led to a formal collaboration, which later included Roland Menzel, a Xerox physicist.

The trio's initial experiments were unsuccessful. For a variety of technical reasons, it proved impractical to continue trying to get iodine to fluoresce. By that time, though, they had done considerable research into fluorescence in general and were not prepared to give up. They tried a different tack. What if there was something already in fingerprints that could be induced to fluoresce if it was excited in the right way with the right light? Their investigation culminated in the discovery that a laser can illuminate many otherwise invisible fingerprints.

Not only does its high-intensity blue-green light detect fresh prints on most surfaces, including human skin, but the researchers found that the laser is also effective on prints that have been exposed to moisture and to extremes in temperature. They placed a fingerprint on a piece of plain white paper and then baked it in an oven at seventy-five degrees Celsius for two weeks. When bombarded with the laser light, it was as clear as it had been originally. They then took the same piece of paper, held it under running water for five minutes and left it to dry at room temperature. When they turned on the laser again, the print was slightly fainter, but still exhibited excellent ridge detail when viewed through special laser goggles. Not so with two traditional chemical techniques: when the same sheet of paper was treated first with ninhydrin and then with silver nitrate, none of the detail necessary for identification was visible. The researchers subsequently found that the laser was equally effective on old fingerprints — for example, on two fourteen-month-old letters and in a book that had not been opened for nine years.

By far the most desirable feature of the technique, now used worldwide, was that it was non-invasive. Laser examinations require no dusting or staining. If they turn up nothing, another method can always be used. And they don't preclude other scientific analyses: a bloodstained knife, for example, can be lasered for prints before it undergoes serology testing.

Within months, the discovery was put to the test. An OPP officer who had heard about the new procedure brought Dalrymple a 7.5-centimetre piece of black electrical tape that had been used to bind a plastic bag full of illegal drugs. Dalrymple knew that the tape would be tricky to laser. Dark objects tend to absorb light, not reflect it; furthermore, a lot of the absorbed energy is converted to heat. If he zapped it too hard, he'd burn the exhibit. But he gave it a shot.

When he examined the tape under the argon-ion laser in the Xerox research centre, he saw the faintest orange fluorescence on the sticky side. "At that point, I couldn't say what it was. I wasn't even sure if I was seeing it." He conferred with Duff and Menzel, and the trio decided that if there was something there, they might be able to capture it on film if they took a time-lapse photograph with the shutter open for an extended period.

In spite of his considerable training and experience in photography, Dalrymple was still guessing when he calculated the exposure times. "When you are talking about light that weak, you can't take a meter reading. None of the normal methods apply. However, after you've been doing this kind of thing for a long time, you develop a gut feeling. And as often as not, you're in the ballpark."

He put a regular 35-millimetre camera on a tripod, set it for one twenty-minute exposure and went for coffee; when he returned, he reset it for forty minutes. He did not really expect to find anything, he admits. "We were just exploring the possibilities." When the three men examined the developed film, staring back at them was the perfect image of a single fingerprint. "There was a little jumping up and down and a little congratulating of each other," says the normally staid researcher.

Up to that point, there had been no physical evidence tying the suspect to the case. "He hadn't even been charged," says Dalrymple. "We introduced the evidence at a preliminary hearing and he subsequently pleaded guilty."

In 1977, the OPP became the first police force in the world to purchase its own laser — a sixteen-watt argon-ion model with a two-metre light tube and a power supply the size of a small filing cabinet. The price tag: $20,000. Soon after, a murderer was convicted when the laser illuminated his fingerprints on a cheap paper napkin found next to the dead body; once again, it was the only physical evidence linking the perpetrator and the crime.

As Dalrymple stands in a large examination room in the OPP laboratory overlooking Toronto's Lakeshore Boulevard, he looks immaculate in a white lab coat worn over a dress shirt and trousers, tie and new brown loafers. Yet his white latex gloves are stained magenta from chemicals as he uses long tweezers to dip $20,000 worth of $20 bills, one by one, into a lasagna-sized pan filled with acrid ninhydrin solution. It will take two days to chemically stain and dry each bill and then develop its prints with heat and humidity.

Dalrymple looks back nearly two decades to the discovery of the new fingerprinting technique and modestly puts it into context for a visitor. Although it has been highly publicized, he says, the laser is not a miracle tool. It can be used on everything, but it is used most often in the lab on plastic bags in which illegal drugs have been packaged and on human skin to detect all forms of trace evidence, from prints and bodily fluids to fibres.

"Ninhydrin is still our bread-and-butter technique," he says. "You can't say one technique is better than the other. They all complement one another and have their own place in our kit."

The laboratory-based laser has led to the development of portable offshoots, which are the biggest boon to forensic investigation since Faulds reported that fingerprints could be picked up at a crime scene. One, called the Luma-Lite, recently invented by another Canadian, John Watkin, at the National Research Council, resembles an aluminum suitcase and costs about $15,000. A less powerful — but at $300 more affordable — alternative is the ultraviolet light. In a darkened room, these new tools can illuminate everything, from the tiniest thread in a carpet to bloodstains under paint.

As well, research in Britain and the United States has enhanced the laser process. Prints that might not otherwise fluoresce can be encouraged to do so if they are first exposed to the fumes of heated Krazy Glue and then treated with a special dye. On some surfaces, notably dark ones, the glue vapours alone are used; they plasticize the prints and turn them white.

In 1989, in northern Alberta, a man was accused of sexually assaulting two young girls in the back of his car; he denied even being with them. RCMP ident officers fumed the entire interior of his car with Krazy Glue and then turned on the Luma-Lite. There, on one of the back windows, was a cluster of tiny fingerprints belonging to one of the victims. When the light was off, they could not be seen.

In British Columbia, a woman was killed by a hit-and-run driver. Police tracked down a suspect, only to find he had washed and waxed his car in the interim. The coverup didn't work. The Luma-Lite picked up a two-millimetre synthetic thread embedded in a tiny nick in the front grille. It was matched to the victim's clothing.

In another case in B.C., minute fibres, which were traced back to the carpet in a rapist's house, were found in his female victim's hair. There is absolutely no chance they would have been found without the Luma-Lite, in the opinion of one of the RCMP ident officers who worked on the case: "This is airborne fluff, the stuff you see when the sun shines brightly through a window. So much of it fluoresces. You pick it up with a piece of Scotch tape and shine the Luma-Lite on it."

Blood does not fluoresce, but under the laser or Luma-Lite, it shows up as a distinct flat black. In a year-old murder case in Prince George, B.C., the Luma-Lite picked up blood that had percolated down through a hardwood floor and, in the same house, bloodstains on a wall that had subsequently been painted.

Finding fingerprints is just the first stage of identifying a perpetrator. No matter how visible and detailed today's high-tech devices make them, prints are meaningless until they are matched to a person. Again, science has made the task a relative breeze. Across Canada, police forces are hooking up to a national computerized fingerprint identification system and electronically filing every print they have. In a mere five minutes, this state-of-the-art system can scan a print, compare it with every one on record across the country, and come up with several possible matches, based on a standard scoring system — a feat that would have been unimaginable when the prints were on paper.

Identifying the perpetrator is just the first step in solving a crime. Proving what happened is the next. Sometimes, this is a straightforward exercise; other times, it is anything but. In death, things are not always as they appear.

Herb LeRoy, now an inspector in charge of research and development in crime-scene examination at the RCMP's Ottawa headquarters, recalls being called out to a possible homicide in Surrey, B.C., in 1990. A woman had been shot in the head while she sat on her bed. Although she was found holding a rifle, there appeared to be two bullet holes in the door behind her. The weapon was bolt-action, not self-loading; therefore, she could not have fired it twice. And there was some suggestion that she and her husband had been arguing.

LeRoy, a man who used to take apart clocks for a hobby, has the dark, handsome good looks of the archetypal Mountie. At the time, he had spent thirteen years as an identification officer with the RCMP in Kamloops and Vancouver — a position that took him to more than 450 homicide scenes. He had joined the force after graduating from university and was one of the first two Mounties trained in bloodstain-pattern analysis. As a specialist, he had been called out to more murders than most ident officers.

"It doesn't get much uglier," he says. "It was a contact wound in which the head literally exploded in a 360-degree radius. It took a minute to get focused on the technical aspects." When he did, he noticed that there was no shadow pattern anywhere in the room. That told him that the woman must have committed suicide. "If someone else had been standing in the room when she was shot, his outline would have shown up on the wall. It would have been like

65

◆

spray-painting the front of a house through a picket fence: you'd see the shadow of the fence on the house."

In short order, LeRoy's theory was confirmed. Behind the door, on the far side of the adjacent room, the regular ident officers found a casing from a copper-jacketed slug embedded in the plaster wall; a hole in a nearby window suggested the actual bullet was somewhere outside, although it was never found: "What happened was the slug hit the head and separated into two pieces. The copper jacket then became as much of a bullet as the lead projectile. Both left the body and went through the door. But there was only one shot."

The bloodstains at this scene required only the trained eye of a seasoned investigator to tell the story. And, until about fifteen years ago, that was all a crime-scene specialist could rely on to re-create an assault or murder. Now, however, a growing number of identification officers are trained, like LeRoy, in a technique that combines their intuition and experience with sound scientific principles from the fields of mathematics, physics and fluid dynamics to determine what happened. Was it suicide or murder? A cold-blooded killing or an act of self-defence?

By examining the shapes, locations and distribution patterns of the blood at a scene, they can often say not only whether a victim was struck more than once — the first blow creates an open wound, subsequent ones spatter the blood — but with what force. If the victim moved between blows, bloodstain experts can also say how many times the person was struck and where he or she was each time.

An early version of the technique gained prominence in 1966. American defence attorney F. Lee Bailey introduced it at the second trial of Sam Sheppard, a California doctor who twelve years earlier had been convicted of bludgeoning to death his wife, Marilyn, in their suburban lakefront home. Two neighbours testified that they had spent the evening with the Sheppards; when they left, shortly after midnight, Sam was asleep on the couch. Three to four hours later, Marilyn was upstairs in their bed when she was struck twenty-seven times with a metallic instrument shaped like a flashlight; the weapon was never found.

Paul Kirk, a criminologist at the University of California, testified that on the door of a wardrobe in the bedroom, he found blood that belonged to neither the victim nor her husband. Furthermore, he said, his analysis of the bloodstains in the room indicated that she had been attacked by a left-handed person with strength "compatible to that of a woman." Even if the weapon had been wielded backhand by a right-handed person, Kirk said, the bloodstains would have been different. Sam Sheppard was right-handed. The jury deliberated for twelve hours before acquitting him.

Herbert MacDonell, a chemist working for the Corning Glass company, followed up on Kirk's research and eventually began offering courses in the technique at Elmira College in New York State. In 1979, LeRoy became one of the first RCMP identification officers to take the course. Three years later, three scientists at Carleton University in Ottawa, with whom the Mounties had subsequently consulted, offered the first of several Canadian courses for the force.

The techniques for interpreting bloodstains are now so refined that instructors at the Ontario Centre of Forensic Sciences, for example, routinely set up mock crime scenes in a paper-covered lecture room using a dye-soaked sponge on the end of a block of wood to simulate a victim's head. Trainees are then invited into the room and asked to re-create the crime.

The basic principle is that the size and shape of blood drops relate directly to the force and angle of a blow. The smaller the spatters of blood, the greater the force of impact. Passive bleeding, in which blood falls freely straight down from a wound, creates round drops; the larger the drops, the farther the blood has fallen. When blood spurts out as a result of a blow, the drops are elliptical; the more acute the trajectory angle, the narrower and longer the drops. At a fifteen-degree angle, they have a very narrow teardrop shape with long tails pointing in the direction in which they travelled.

Determining the exact angle is where the mathematics comes in. Take a long teardrop-shaped stain, for example. The analysts measure it at its longest and widest parts and then divide the width by the length; the sine of that number is the angle of impact. "It's a simple matter of finding the sine through tables or having the computer do it," says LeRoy. "Once we get that, I can then say, for example, the stain struck the wall at thirty degrees and it was coming from this direction."

It is the patterns of drops, though, that really tell the story. By repeating the same calculation with all of the distinctive bloodstains in each cluster, and then doing a little number-crunching with the computer, LeRoy can determine within centimetres where the angles converge and, therefore, where the blood source was when it was struck. "Generally, I can't say what the blood source was," he says. "But if the guy wasn't bleeding anywhere else but the head, common sense prevails."

Being able to say how many times a person was struck can be particularly useful in differentiating between crimes of passion and cold-blooded assaults, says LeRoy. "It is some sort of defence in court if I say I went off my noodle because of something you said and killed you with a shovel in one blow. But if through bloodstains it can be shown that you ran all over the yard while I beat you over a period of five minutes, sometime during that period, the court would expect me to have come to my senses."

In one such case in Port Alberni, B.C., LeRoy says a man admitted getting into a fight with an elderly male neighbour in the old man's apartment. However, he steadfastly maintained that he hit him only once with a ballpeen hammer and when he left, the victim was not seriously hurt.

"When I arrived," says LeRoy, "I found impact spatters all over the bedroom. They were also wiping patterns and passive pooling on the floor. I was ultimately able to say that the fellow received a minimum of three to five blows while he was on the bed and that he was dragged from there onto the floor where the beating continued. He was left on the floor and under his own steam crawled back up onto the bed."

When the case was tried, the defence lawyer challenged LeRoy's testimony, saying there was no way he could know which blow came first — or even if the blows were delivered on the same day. The Mountie replied that the scenario was based on logical inference and supporting facts. The judge agreed with his re-creation.

In a similar case in 1989 in the West End of Vancouver, a man who said he was heterosexual admitted killing a gay man with whom he had been staying. He argued, however, that he should not be held responsible because he was in a blind rage at the time. The gay man had picked him up in a bar, he said, and taken him back to his luxury apartment. After living together for a week or so with no sexual relations, he awoke one morning to find the gay man sexually assaulting him. He said he flipped out and did not remember what happened in the brief time it took to kill him.

The story that emerged from the bloodstains was quite different. LeRoy's analysis indicated that the initial fight did occur in the bedroom. However, diluted blood in the shower suggested that the victim, apparently believing he was out of danger, went into the bathroom to clean up. A second fight erupted there, he was fatally stabbed, and he crawled out into the hallway, where he died.

Sometimes a perpetrator will admit that he assaulted someone but claim it was in self-defence; here, too, bloodstains can be used to sort out the truth because they indicate the positions of the assailant and victim. It is pretty hard to argue self-defence if bloodstain patterns prove that the victim was lying on the floor when he was struck.

At his first course in New York, LeRoy says, he was taught to do all of the work at the scene. That involved actually running strings out from the spatters in each cluster to find the points of convergence. "It was just a nightmare and it was not accurate. The strings sagged, people stepped on them." But, he says, "it's great for a visual aid."

Now the Mounties do the analysis back at the detachment. At the scene, they lay out a grid, establishing an x and y axis by running one tape measure vertically up the wall and another horizontally. Then they pin a different letter on each significant cluster and photograph everything. Later, they blow up the photographs and determine the trajectory and convergence of the stains on a drafting board with the aid of a special computer program developed in collaboration with the scientists at Carleton University.

"Time is of the essence when you are doing this sort of thing," says LeRoy. In murder investigations, there is a whole team of individuals lined up behind the identification officers to start their jobs — at the scene, the morgue and the lab. One of these is the forensic dentist, who often assumes the responsibility of identifying unknown individuals — like the body that was buried twice — who can no longer be identified visually or from fingerprints.

DENTAL SLEUTHS

IN 1972, VANCOUVER dentist Larry Cheevers was recruited into the grisly business of identifying human remains and analyzing bite marks on rape and murder victims. A native of Galway, Ireland, he graduated from the University of Dublin and worked for three years in England and South Africa before moving to Canada. After obtaining his doctorate in dental surgery at the University of Toronto, he opted for the temperate climate of the West Coast to set up practice.

One of his first patients was Bart Bastien, the coroner who subsequently established British Columbia's world-class forensic identification unit. Cheevers says Bastien seemed nervous in the dental chair; in an attempt to relax him, Cheevers asked about his work.

Each province has its own coroner's system. In Ontario, coroners are doctors; in Quebec, they are lawyers. And in British Columbia, they are laypersons who bring with them a variety of backgrounds. Bart Bastien, for example, has been dealing with dead bodies since the age of eleven, when he began working at a funeral parlour after school, first answering phones and cutting the grass, and then helping to embalm the cadavers. It never occurred to him that it was a bizarre way for an adolescent to make money. "It was a job," he says. "I've always looked at this as a job." In 1955, he began transporting bodies; he went on to work as a morgue attendant, pathologist's assistant, coroner's technician and, finally, coroner.

Like all coroners, Bastien's primary responsibility is to investigate unexplained deaths. Part of that job is determining the identity of the deceased. As he sat in Cheevers's dental chair, Bastien explained that he was periodically called upon to remove the teeth from unknown bodies in the morgue so they could be identified later from dental records, their families could be notified and a death certificate could be issued. Cheevers, who had studied forensic odontology in Ireland, recalls casually mentioning, "If you ever need a hand . . ."

A couple of days later, Bastien took him up on his offer. The decomposed body of a fifteen-year-old girl had been found in Stanley Park. She had been killed six months earlier by a blow to the head with a rock. Cheevers identified the victim, the murderer was convicted and, soon afterwards, the B.C. Coroners Service established a forensic identification unit with Bastien as its full-time head and Cheevers, who is paid on a fee-for-service basis, as chief of forensic odontology for the province.

Larry Cheevers was twenty-nine years old when he met Bastien just over two decades ago. Since then, the pair have worked together on more than two thousand cases; they have also become good friends. Although they are virtual opposites in personality, they have made a good team. "We are like a Laurel and Hardy act," says Cheevers. "Bart is the best right-hand man, a perfect example of what a good civil servant is." Cheevers, a tall, lean man whose short salt-and-pepper hair and thick moustache give him the appearance of the stereotypical detective, is dynamic, passionate in his views and generally outspoken; Bastien is relatively quiet, conservative and cautious and, according to Cheevers, has often kept him from "going out on a limb." In their affinity for work, though, the two men are identical.

Bastien has been on call 365 days a year for virtually his entire career. His curly, once auburn hair and close-cropped beard are now grey and the wrinkles deeper behind his wire-rim glasses, but he continues to drive himself. Although he officially retired in 1993, he is still on call to the "outside experts" at murder scenes. And he can still be found most mornings by eight-thirty either at the morgue or at the same desk in his old office in Burnaby, trying to identify unknown cadavers.

Cheevers is equally driven. He jokes that he needs roller skates to keep up with the demands of a dental practice that, as a result of his extraordinary energy, has burgeoned over the years, earning him a comfortable living. He lives with his wife and two daughters in an Arthur Erickson–styled mansion in the heart of Vancouver's posh Shaughnessy neighbourhood, drives a new Mercedes, employs a maid and a gardener and belongs to two country clubs. Yet he continues to devote considerable time outside the traditional confines of his profession to forensic work, which offers little glamour and even less money.

Over the years, he and Bastien have met several times a week, usually before regular working hours in the morgue at Vancouver General Hospital, where they have done most of their work on the bodies. And many a dental riddle has been solved at their regular noon-hour haunt, a greasy-spoon delicatessen called Tim's, half a block from Cheevers's Grandview-area office. One involved a middle-aged woman who had been sexually assaulted and beaten to death while taking a shortcut through a schoolyard late at night. When the forensic pathologist was doing the autopsy, she found a strange semi-circular bruise on the back of the woman's neck; Cheevers later confirmed that the injury had all the characteristics of half a bite mark. But how could that be? Where was the other arch?

As Cheevers and Bastien bolted sandwiches and rehashed the facts of the case, the coroner wondered aloud whether the crime-scene photographs, which he had with him, would help. No, Cheevers told him, they wouldn't tell them anything. Bastien pulled them out anyway. There, lying on the ground in one of the shots, was a denture. Cheevers asked whether the woman had false teeth. Yes, Bastien replied. That's it, the dentist said. In all likelihood, the victim was not bitten by her assailant at all. Her false teeth were probably knocked out during the struggle and she was pinned down on one half. When Cheevers later compared the bite-mark impression he had taken after the autopsy with the woman's dentures, his theory checked out.

Given the ghoulish nature of the job, it's not surprising that Cheevers's attempts over the years to recruit colleagues have been largely unsuccessful. Some would-be apprentices have passed out on their first trip to the morgue. But it's not just working on corpses that forensic dentists have to be able to handle. They must also accept that their personal and office time could be interrupted at any minute by a call to duty. And there may be no time to recover from the ordeal.

In February 1978, for example, Cheevers and Bastien were called to the scene of the Cranbrook air disaster, in which forty-three people died when their plane crashed in a heavy snowstorm. In a washroom next to the morgue storage room in the local hospital — the only quiet place large enough to accommodate them — they worked alone through the night, charting and x-raying the victims' teeth so they could be positively identified from records supplied by their dentists.

As he worked, Cheevers noticed that the passengers' teeth had turned pink, a phenomenon that has also been observed in drowning and hanging victims and in those who have died from carbon monoxide poisoning or in fires. The theory is that when breathing is obstructed, the blood pressure rises and a thin membrane inside the teeth ruptures, causing haemoglobin to be pushed through the internal dentine, which turns the teeth pink. The only exceptions were the pilot and copilot. Cheevers reasoned that they had been killed on impact, whereas the passengers had died of smoke inhalation. "They came down stunned," he suggests, "but they had survived. If there had been good fire protection, if there was an ambulance present, if they had been able to extract those bodies, I am quite sure that most of those people would have survived."

Cheevers did not make his thoughts public. His job was to identify the bodies, Bastien reminded him, not to make assumptions about the cause of death. It was probably the right decision, he says now, given that the pink-teeth phenomenon remains hypothetical. "Imagine the controversy I would have raised by saying something like that."

He and Bastien worked all night long on the Cranbrook emergency. With no sleep, they caught a return flight to Vancouver in the morning. It arrived at noon, giving Cheevers just enough time to get back to his office to meet a patient at 1 p.m.

Criminal investigations require more time than mass disasters both to prepare for court and to testify at preliminary hearings and trials. Furthermore, it is not uncommon for judicial proceedings to be cancelled and rescheduled. Nonetheless, several years ago, Cheevers was finally successful in persuading David Sweet, a member of the dental faculty at the University of British Columbia, to join the odontology team. Both accept the sacrifices of the job for the rewards, which Cheevers lists as the opportunity to serve the community at large, satisfying scientific curiosity and excitement. "There can be no doubt that you get a positive adrenalin rush when you can assist in what may seem to be a hopeless case." For these dental sleuths, each mystery they help unravel is as unique as the set of teeth involved.

Although identifying human remains is the bread-and-butter work of forensic odontology, experts like Larry Cheevers are sometimes asked to identify the perpetrator of a crime through bite marks. In some cases, a single bruise has led to the conviction of a murderer.

In December 1988, in a homicidal frenzy, someone beat a woman, strangled her and then threw her body out a window before dragging it into a swamp behind the Newton Inn in Surrey, B.C., where it was discovered later the same day.

Although the body was covered in cuts and bruises, the contusions and abrasions around the neck formed a linear pattern characteristic of ligature strangulation. At the autopsy the next morning, the cause of death was confirmed; the bruises on the woman's throat extended deep into the tissues above a U-shaped bone called the hyoid, located at the base of the tongue. As well, the right main chamber of her heart was greatly dilated, which is typical of airway obstruction. The forensic pathologist also determined from microscopic examination of the bruises that the woman had been beaten fifteen to thirty minutes before she died.

What piqued the pathologist's curiosity, though, was one particular bruise above the victim's right breast. To the untrained eye, the contusion would not appear significantly different from those on the rest of the body. However, to the pathologist and to Bastien, who attended the post-mortem, the bruise looked like it could be a bite mark.

As strange as it may seem, some killers, especially those whose crimes involve a sexual element, bite their victims. One of the most infamous of these cases involved Ted Bundy, the American serial killer who got away with murdering and mutilating at least thirty women before forensic dentists matched an impression of his teeth to a deep bite mark on the buttock of a Florida sorority member.

Bite marks in inanimate objects have been accepted into evidence by the courts for many years; a burglar was convicted in England in 1906 after leaving a partially eaten piece of cheese at a crime scene. However, investigations involving bite marks on human skin are fairly recent; in Canadian courts, such evidence has been accepted for only the past two decades.

When someone bites a piece off an apple, the outsides of the teeth leave an impression on the fruit. Conversely, if a person bites another person, the insides of the teeth leave marks. Both kinds of evidence can be quickly lost. Foodstuffs are prone to dehydrate if they are not kept refrigerated in an airtight container until dental impressions can be taken. Bite marks on skin change colour and shape over time, even after death; skin distorts as a result of movement and its own elasticity and eventually the subcutaneous haemorrhage, or bruise, fades away completely.

Bastien wasted no time in calling Cheevers and Sweet that Saturday morning about the bruise above the right breast of the young female murder victim. The two dentists arrived at the morgue at ten and, after confirming that the injury was characteristic of a recent bite mark, they set about collecting the evidence. First the bruise was photographed, using various lighting and exposures, alongside a millimetre ruler for scale. Next, Sweet cleaned the skin with sterile water, using cotton swabs that were allowed to dry and then placed in a test tube for serological testing. (In 80 percent of the population, an individual's saliva contains substances that correspond to his blood type; since traces of saliva are often left at the site of bite marks, this evidence can further implicate or eliminate a suspect.)

The third step was to obtain a model of the bite mark for later comparison, if possible, with the suspect's dentition, or teeth. If the perpetrator's teeth have created identations on the skin, a physical cast of the injury is taken; silicone or rubber-based dental material is applied to the area, backed with plastic-mesh orthopaedic tape for support. The trickiest part of this procedure, particularly when the body has been refrigerated, can be to get the skin to the right temperature for the mould to set. Cheevers recalls one instance in which the decomposing body had been frozen. He and Bastien tried to warm it up by placing heat lamps over it; however, to their dismay, the putrefaction process resumed right before their eyes. They quickly removed the lamps and waited another two and a half hours for their cast.

When Cheevers and Sweet examined the bite mark under a microscope, they could detect no identation on the skin from the perpetrator's teeth; therefore, taking a standard impression would be pointless. Instead, they opted for a technique developed by Montreal forensic dentist Robert Dorion called transillumination. This involves cutting out the bite mark and the surrounding tissue, fixing it in a chemical preservative and then viewing it on a light box. When the underlying light shines up through the specimen, the outline of the bite mark is clearly delineated. Cheevers explains it this way: Normally, looking down at a bite mark in skin is akin to looking through water at the blurry image of a coin at the bottom of a swimming pool. Transillumination is equivalent to putting on a pair of goggles and swimming down to have a look.

When employing transillumination, forensic dentists have to take great care not to distort the bite mark as they remove it. To stabilize the tissue, they first glue a plastic ring — actually a thin slice of PVC pipe — to the surface of the skin surrounding the bite mark. This is gently sutured in place. Then they cut vertically around the perimeter of the ring and horizontally under the fatty bottom layer of skin to remove the three-dimensional piece of tissue. To prevent the specimen from decomposing or distorting, it is preserved in fixative for ten hours before being mounted on the light box and photographed.

At three o'clock that afternoon, with the preliminary stage of the work completed, Cheevers turned his attention to the next hurdle. Photographs of a bite mark on their own would mean nothing without an impression of the suspect's teeth. The RCMP had taken into custody the last person seen with the young woman before she was found dead, Aaron Tammie. There was only one glitch: whereas in the United States investigators can request a search warrant from a judge that allows them to obtain dental impressions from an accused person who refuses to co-operate, and anaesthetize him if he continues to resist, in Canada, suspects must give their permission before impressions can be taken. This situation frustrates and infuriates Cheevers, given that in this country a person suspected of drunk driving can be forced to provide breath or blood samples. "Because of some ridiculous concept that we are abrogating someone's rights, we have to go in and say, 'I'm a nice guy, would you mind biting on this.'"

Suspects had been known to consent, however. And since there was no harm in asking, Cheevers and Bastien set off for the RCMP detachment in Surrey where Tammie was being held. To their surprise, the accused man was extremely co-operative and he agreed to have photographs and wax impressions taken of his teeth. Those in hand, Cheevers and Bastien headed straight for the dentist's office, where they spent an hour and a half making the mould out of dental stone.

It was long past dinnertime when the pair finally headed for home. It had been a long day and would have been gruelling under the best of circumstances, starting as it did with five straight hours of standing on the cold, hard morgue floor; but Cheevers had the added burden of a herniated disc he had suffered in a car accident a few days earlier. He had been in considerable pain all day and had been able to get around only using a walking stick.

The effort paid off, though. Even before he had transilluminated the bite mark, Cheevers was fairly certain, after comparing the photographs of Tammie's teeth with those of the bite mark, that they had a match. In official language, "there were enough points of similarity between them to merit further investigation." Cheevers was careful, however, to avoid giving a precursory opinion before he had examined in detail both the pattern and the measurements of the bite mark and the moulds and photographs taken from Tammie. "You have got to be very methodical about these things," he says. "It takes time. But it's my neck that is going to be on the line when I go to court. I've got to be sure that in ten years' time, nobody is going to be able to come around and say, what you said was not right. I am kind of proselytizing a particular science." There have been occasions when Cheevers's findings, like those of other forensic scientists, have met with not only intense scrutiny but scepticism.

Awareness of the potential of dental identification has grown over the years, boosted in part by publicity surrounding such cases as the identification in Brazil in 1985 of the remains of infamous Nazi war criminal Josef Mengele, the so-called Angel of Death at Auschwitz. A decade earlier, however, forensic dentistry still had not been wholeheartedly embraced by everyone in the judicial community. Cheevers specifically remembers his first case, when he confirmed the identity of the teenaged girl who had been found in Stanley Park. "The coroner in charge didn't believe me. He thought I was talking through the top of my hat. I actually had to take the x-rays to him and show him."

Even today, professionals within this small discipline — there are only a handful of qualified forensic odontologists in Canada — must overcome ignorance and naivety about what their science can do.

Bite marks commonly go unrecognized in criminal investigations, Cheevers says, and perpetrators of violent crimes, particularly child abuse, are going free because of it. "The average person does not recognize bite marks. If they saw one they would say, 'That's not a bite mark. It's just a bruise.'"

It takes training, experience and a certain amount of intuition to differentiate between a simple bruise and the marks caused by teeth, and persistence to prove it. "A lot of the time, I'm like a blind man looking for the door. I know the evidence is there. I just have to feel around until I come up with it."

When Cheevers and Sweet transilluminated the bruise excised from the body of the Surrey murder victim, they were astonished at the clarity. What had appeared as a dif-

fuse discolouration of the skin surface was suddenly trans-
formed into a well-demarcated bite mark. The contour of
the inside of the teeth was particularly distinct. When they
traced the inside of Tammie's dentition onto a piece of
acetate and projected it to scale onto a white wall, it fit the
outline of the bite mark like a glove.

Phone calls to colleagues across the continent revealed
that the technique of transillumination, although widely
known, had not yet been introduced in court. Cheevers
made arrangements for the images of both the dentition and
the bite mark to be computer enhanced, using methods
honed by American forensic dentists during the Ted Bundy
investigation. With these finely detailed slides, two video
cameras and a mixing box, they superimposed the images,
fading the bruise in and out of the teeth. It was a perfect fit.
"We showed it to the RCMP and it blew them away," says
Cheevers.

Aaron Tammie must have had a similar reaction
because he pleaded guilty after viewing the evidence at a
preliminary hearing. Cheevers admits he was disappointed
that the case did not go to trial. "I felt like Reggie Jackson.
I'm called up to bat the ball, the bases are loaded, and the
bloody game is called."

It's cases like these that have kept the sociable dentist
buoyed during twenty-two years of working on bite marks
and identifying bodies that are too badly mutilated or
decomposed to be visually recognized. Cheevers says he can
usually turn his mind off to the horror he sees by concentrat-
ing on the intellectual challenge before him. But in many
bite mark investigations the victim is a child, and these cases
are always painful. "I don't go around crying or getting sick

at the side of the road like some do, but it upsets me. I'm a parent myself."

At seven-thirty on Monday morning in March 1987, Cindy Harker went in to wake up her young daughter, Stacie, and discovered that the three-year-old was not in her bedroom and there were what appeared to be bloodstains on her sheets. When a frantic search of the house and the immediate Kamloops, B.C., neighbourhood turned up no sign of the little girl, her mother called the police. Stacie's father, Bob, drove to the home of a long-time family friend, James Patrick Jones, to ask him to join in the search. The night before, Jones had visited with the Harkers and Stacie's uncle before falling asleep in their living room.

The thirty-six-year-old attractive, clean-cut former television cameraman readily agreed to help. The two men had just returned to the Harker home when the police arrived.

One of the RCMP investigating officers, Cpl. Frank Boyle, later told reporters that he was immediately suspicious of Jones. "He exhibited several signs that made me nervous. He was also excessively co-operative." Boyle also noticed Jones trying to hide a bruise between the thumb and index finger on one hand.

As searchers combed the banks of the nearby North Thompson River, Boyle and his partner took Jones to a lounge in a local motor inn to interrogate him in a more relaxed atmosphere. At one point, they suggested that the mark on his hand was the result of a bite. Jones said they were probably right; he later gave Boyle permission to take an impression of it.

Stacie Harker's body had yet to be found when Boyle

turned over the exhibit to Cheevers for a proper mould to be made. However, pieces of the child's night clothing had been discovered near the shore and there were drag marks leading from the bank to the water's edge. For the next five days, police divers scoured the river bottom, while a search-and-rescue boat dragged the dark waters; police dogs and a helicopter were also brought in to help. The body was finally found the following Saturday morning in a shallow backeddy, where it had been shielded from the river current by a sandbar.

Even seasoned police officers at the scene were obviously distressed as the tiny body was loaded into the coroner's vehicle. Kamloops regional coroner Bob Graham announced to the shocked community that the autopsy would not be done locally. Instead, the body would be flown to Vancouver, widely recognized as one of the foremost forensic centres in the country.

The post-mortem determined that the child had been badly bruised and sexually assaulted, and the cause of death was drowning. When it was completed, Cheevers was called in to take impressions of the child's teeth.

When Cheevers later compared computer-enhanced images of the victim's dentition to the bite mark on Jones's hand, he concluded they were a match. In fighting back, Stacie Harker did more than just identify her killer, however. She enabled Cheevers to deduce, both from the bite mark and the injuries to her lower lip, how she had been restricted during the assault and, by extension, how she had been assaulted. As he explained his findings at the preliminary hearing, Cheevers says, "I could see everyone thinking how could he deduce so much on the basis of a bite mark. But I can remember Jones looking up at me and his eyes opening up. I knew I had struck a chord." When the hearing was over, Jones pleaded guilty and was sentenced to twenty-five years in prison.

Teeth have been used as a personal signature for centuries. Knights in the Middle Ages are said to have bitten the sealing wax on their last wills and testaments before they embarked on a crusade to make a distinctive imprint that could not be tampered with or faked. Because teeth are more apt than other tissues in the human body to survive fire, trauma and decomposition, they have also long been used to identify disfigured victims.

In North America, the origin of forensic odontology is commonly traced back to 1776. That year, Paul Revere identified the body of Gen. Joseph Warren almost a year after he had been killed by the British at Bunkerhill, stripped of his possessions and buried in a mass grave. Revere, a silversmith who operated a dental practice in Boston, made the identification on the basis of a denture he had crafted for Warren from a walrus tusk and silver wires.

Although the methods employed today are considerably more scientific, the principle of dental identification remains the same. Every set of teeth is different and becomes increasingly personalized through wear and tear, disease and dental restorations. Adults start out with thirty-two teeth, each of which has five surfaces that can be altered by cavities or fillings. Considering that the dental materials themselves can range from gold, silver and cement to caps of various designs — and that certain teeth may be missing — the various combinations and permutations of the final dental pattern represent a degree of specificity for one individual that can approach astronomical proportions.

In some criminal investigations, Larry Cleevers says, teeth can be as useful as fingerprints. To the trained eye, they can reveal a multitude of facts, including a person's age, size, sex, race, occupation and socio-economic status. When the police are dealing with partial skeletal remains, the teeth may be the only means available for obtaining this information.

A British dentist first proposed during the industrial revolution in England that teeth were a much more reliable indicator of age than height. As a result, the British Parliament passed a law in 1837 requiring children to have a certificate from a dentist confirming that they were at least thirteen years old before they could be sent to work in the cotton mills or coal mines.

Today, dentists can even estimate the age of a foetus after two months' gestation by removing a tooth bud and staining the germinating tooth. Between birth and age twenty-one, the state of the exfoliation and eruption of the primary and permanent teeth allows dentists to determine an individual's age to within six months or a year. In an older person, they can often estimate age to within five years by assessing various changes within the tissues that surround and support the teeth, including the degree of wear on the crown, the transparency of the root dentine, the shape of the pulp chamber and how much the gums have receded.

Forensic dentists can also say something about an individual's stature — the larger the person, the greater the tooth and root size — and up to five months after death, they can determine someone's sex by grinding down the dentine and checking the chromosomes. To render an opinion about race, they usually need more than one tooth, although shovel-shaped incisors are common in East Asian and native North American peoples. There are also certain patterns of wear that are characteristic, for example, of musicians who play wind instruments, carpenters who hold nails between their teeth or seamstresses who do the same with pins. And socio-economic status can sometimes be gauged by the repair work that has been done on a person's teeth.

Cheevers recalls one case in which he was called in to the morgue on his way back from a trip to Whistler, literally arriving in his ski gear. His help was needed to identify the badly decomposed and naked bodies of two women believed to have been murdered. His initial assessments later proved uncannily accurate. He estimated the first woman's age to be twenty-one and said it was obvious to him from the huge exposed cavities in her mouth that she was a drug addict; it is the only way she would have been able to stand the pain. The second woman he judged was twenty-four years old and, on the basis of the bridgework that had been done on her teeth, came from a middle-class background and looked after herself. "This isn't something you learn at university, but after twenty-two years' experience, you have an intuitive eye that tells you what's going on."

The first major use of dental identification in a mass disaster in Canada was in September 1949, when the SS *Noronic*, the flagship of the Canada Steamship Lines, which was tied up to the pier in Toronto harbour with over seven hundred passengers on board, burst into flames in the middle of the night. The fire spread so quickly that dozens of passengers were trapped in the hallways and stairs below deck. Forty-one dentists participated in identifying the 188 victims. In a report on the operation, two of the dentists noted that their task would have been less arduous if all dentists compiled and maintained accurate records of their patients. The criticism is still being levelled in North America today.

During the 1980s, forensic odontologists in the United States were called upon to identify the decomposing remains of thirty-six of the forty victims of a serial killer operating in the Green River area of Seattle. They reported that they had to contend with incomplete or poor-quality dental records, inconsistent charting and recording, and sporadic missing-person reports. As a result, they said, tracing the identity of the victims consumed substantial resources.

In Canada, says Cheevers, forensic dentists face additional problems created by the computer program for dental files established in 1978 by the RCMP for the national communications system of the Canadian Police Information Centre (CPIC). In principle, every time a person is reported missing, his or her dental records should be put into the system for comparison with any unidentified bodies that are recovered. That does not happen routinely, says Cheevers, which means, at best, that expensive and time-consuming traditional investigation methods have to be used to identify an individual and, at worst, that a corpse remains unidentified. But even if every dentist in the country co-operated fully in the program, the RCMP is not equipped to use their information to its fullest.

No dentist was ever consulted when the dental record program was established, Cheevers says, and for years it was virtually useless. In response to pressure from the odonotology section of the Canadian Society of Forensic Science, spearheaded by Cheevers when he was chairman, some improvements were finally made in the late 1980s. But by then the system was obsolete: unlike newer programs used in other countries, it cannot sift its data to produce information on treatments to a single tooth or a small section of teeth, which might be sufficiently unique to identify a person and may be all that is left when skeletal remains have been destroyed or scattered by animals. "If the RCMP were suddenly told that they had to have all ten fingerprints to identify a suspect, they would say that is ridiculous," says Cheevers. "But they are imposing that restriction on dentists with their dental program."

Although there have been rumours within the B.C. forensic community that, as a result of Cheevers's tenacity, the RCMP is updating the CPIC dental program, Cheevers still thinks the biggest obstacle is money. "The RCMP conquered the West on borrowed horses and they are still borrowing today. That's what they do with all their outside experts. They have to realize that if they want proper outside assistance they are going to have to pay for it."

The problem is compounded, he says, by the insular nature of the RCMP. Whereas the FBI has two full-time forensic dentists who provide input on matters such as computerized dental records, the RCMP still thinks that "every country's police force is required to reinvent the wheel."

"They are a tremendous police force," says Cheevers. "But they were conceived in the nineteenth century and it's going to be awfully difficult to drag them into the twenty-first century. They were set up to go out and conquer lawlessness. That's okay when a guy's got a gun and he's robbing a bank. It's simple and logical. The toughest guy won and the RCMP was the toughest guy. But that isn't crime any more.

"With the expanding scientific aspect of investigations, they've got to be up there on the leading edge all the time."

Part of staying at the forefront for the B.C. Coroners Service has been to increase the number of the outside experts it has incorporated into its team approach to investigating unnatural deaths. Coroners need to know not only who died but how.

THE
ELOQUENT
DEAD

I N 1983, A YEAR AFTER
Clifford Olson was convicted of murdering eleven children
in British Columbia, the B.C. Coroners Service appointed a
chief forensic pathologist. Before then, forensic autopsies in
Vancouver were performed at the old city morgue on an ad
hoc basis by several pathologists from the Lions Gate
Hospital; the doctors worked separately, after hours, and did
not attend crime scenes. The appointment of James Ferris
signalled a growing awareness of the significant contribution
that specially trained dentists, doctors and academics could
make in solving complex homicides, particularly when they
were permanent members of the investigating team.

Ferris — who was concurrently appointed professor of forensic pathology at the University of British Columbia and head of forensic pathology at Vancouver General Hospital, or VGH — had already been involved in hundreds of murder cases in Britain and Canada and had earned a reputation for impeccable integrity and meticulous work habits. Morgue attendants at VGH quickly learned not to touch his autopsy knives, which, unlike most pathologists, he sharpens himself. "I have a thing about my knives," he says. "I have my own. I keep them in a case and I don't let anyone else touch them. You don't cut yourself on a sharp knife."

Ferris was imbued with discipline at a young age. A native of Belfast, he spent his adolescence at Campbell College, an Anglican boarding school. At the age of thirteen, he enrolled in the army cadets and later spent time in the university officers training corps as well as in the territorial army reserve in England, where he achieved the rank of major.

In the mid-1960s, he was a medical resident in Belfast when he decided to take up pathology because, although it seems incongruous, he was squeamish around blood. He had been known to faint in the operating room, yet he found that at an autopsy he became so absorbed in the problem at hand that he could ignore the fact that he was cutting up a body. Particularly engrossing for him were the forensic cases, which he did initially simply because no one else wanted to do them. His colleagues preferred clinical pathology, in which autopsies are performed to study the disease process in individuals who die of natural causes. Forensic postmortems, on the other hand, are conducted to determine the cause and circumstances of unnatural deaths. At what angle did the bullet enter the body? Did the victim drown or was she suffocated and then placed in water? Ferris loved the mystery, which he attributes to his Irish background: "We were brought up steeped in mythology with legends and secret tunnels in abbeys, and ghosts that appear at certain crossroads at certain times of the year."

When he had sufficient training to begin going to homicide scenes, he admits that he even enjoyed aspects of that part of the job. He occasionally had to pull over to the side of the road to be sick after attending a particularly gruesome scene, though for the most part, he says, "I enjoyed the status, which was maybe just my perception. There was always a crowd and they'd whisper, 'Here comes the pathologist.'" The excitement was also appealing. "I've always driven sports cars and have followed motor and motorcycle racing for as long as I can remember. I was medical officer at Mosport Park racing circuit near Toronto. The ultimate thrill, though, is being able to contribute positively. There are not many people whose jobs give them both elements."

By scouting a homicide scene, forensic pathologists can determine whether there is anything — from insects to the surface on which the body landed — that might have caused injuries unrelated to the assault. They may be able to tell the police whether a suspicious-looking death is in fact a murder. A drunk who is dead following a fist fight, for example, may actually have fallen after the scuffle, causing his own death. And Ferris has been known to go to great lengths to make this point. In one instance in Vancouver, he re-enacted the first stage of a suicide to prove to the police that a man had not been pushed off a bridge. By climbing over the side and hanging by his fingers, as the victim would have done before he dropped to his death, Ferris sustained the same scrapes on his hands and wrists.

On another occasion, his forensic pathology training in injury interpretation uncovered a murder that otherwise probably would never have been detected. Ferris was on his way into the autopsy room in the basement morgue at VGH when he happened to walk by the body of an elderly patient who had died in hospital, supposedly of natural causes. No autopsy had been scheduled. However, Ferris noticed significant bruising on the woman's face and neck, which he reported to the coroner. "Oh, the doctor said that woman had terminal cancer," the coroner informed him. "She may well have," Ferris replied, "but she's sure got marks and haemorrhages that I don't like." An autopsy was ordered. Ferris found that the woman's neck had been broken. Her nephew was subsequently charged with killing her.

Because forensic pathologists are trained both as laboratory scientists and medical practitioners, with special emphasis on the interpretation of injuries and the causes of death, they are perceived to have a broader perspective than other forensic scientists. As a result, they are sometimes asked to give an overview of the scientific findings in complicated cases. More often than not, though, they are asked after the fact, as independent experts, to review old cases because of a dispute over the validity or relevance of the physical evidence presented at the initial trial. Roughly a third of the thousand-plus homicide cases on which Ferris has worked over the years have been reviews. The most exciting for him was the famous 1980 Australian case of the dingo that may have killed a baby.

Lindy Chamberlain claimed that her infant daughter,

Azaria, was seized by a wild dog while the family was camping near Ayers Rock in the country's red-sand outback. The mother said her baby was sleeping inside their tent at the popular tourist spot. Nearby, she was preparing dinner for her husband, Michael, a minister for the Seventh-Day Adventist Church, and their two young sons. When the pastor said he heard Azaria crying, Lindy went to investigate. She said that through the darkness, she could see a dingo running out of the tent shaking its head. Moments later, she discovered the infant was missing.

Hundreds of volunteers with torches combed the rocky slopes through the night. An official search continued the next day. A week later, Azaria's bloodstained jumpsuit and underclothing were discovered five kilometres from the campsite. There was no sign, however, of the matinee jacket she had been wearing over the jumpsuit. Her body was never found.

The media pounced on the case, and news of it reverberated around the world. When reporters quoted the parents as saying they accepted the tragedy as the will of God, scepticism and speculation grew. Gossips whispered (incorrectly) that the name Azaria meant sacrifice in the wilderness.

At a televised inquest six months later in Alice Springs, the presiding judge ruled that neither parent was responsible for the death of the child. He noted that a forensic dentist, who reported that there was no evidence that the rips on the infant's jumpsuit were caused by a dingo, was not an expert in bite marks. The dentist sought a second opinion from James Cameron, a forensic pathologist in London, England. When Cameron also challenged the theory that the baby had been taken by a dingo, a second inquest was held and a trial ordered.

On September 13, 1982, as the trial began in Darwin, the Crown attorney told the jury that the dingo story was a fanciful invention. What really happened, he said, was that Lindy cut Azaria's throat in the front seat of the family car and hid her body in a camera bag until she could dispose of it; she then cleaned up the blood, sprinkling some of it around the tent, and began her charade. Later, she cut the infant's jumpsuit and discarded it near a dingo's lair.

The Crown called on scientists who explained how their tests supported the theory. The experts testified that they found bloodstains under the dashboard of the car and impressions of bloodstained fingers on the infant's jumpsuit. Their tests showed the damage to the garment was consistent with cuts made by scissors and that there was very little blood in the tent and no traces of saliva on the garment to indicate it had been in a dingo's jaws.

Qualified witnesses for the defence gave conflicting evidence in support of the dingo theory. Jury members were shown photographs in which a doll's head, the same size as Azaria's, easily fit into a dingo's jaws. They watched a video-taped experiment in which a dingo quickly removed a baby's jumpsuit from a kid goat. They were told that it was possible that the animal bit into the baby's head in such a way that its teeth plugged the scalp wounds, preventing significant bleeding in the tent; it was also feasible that the dog's saliva had been confined to the outer matinee jacket, which had not been recovered. Finally, they were reminded, the Crown had introduced no weapon and had suggested no motive for murder.

The trial lasted seven weeks. The jury deliberated for six and a half hours before unanimously deciding that the Chamberlains were guilty: Lindy of murdering her daughter and Michael of being an accessory after the fact. The judge sentenced the mother to life imprisonment with hard labour; the father received a sentence of eighteen months, which was suspended in view of the family's young sons.

Two subsequent appeals were rejected, but doubts about the case persisted. In 1986, five and a half years after Azaria disappeared, her matinee jacket was discovered in the sand near the body of a British climber killed in a fall, casting doubt on evidence presented at the original trial. Lindy was released from prison and a royal commission was established to review the case. In 1987, the Chamberlains were exonerated. In 1990, they accepted a settlement from the Northern Territory government for their legal bills, and in 1992, they were awarded almost a million dollars in compensation for wrongful conviction.

Public fascination with the case continues. It has been the subject of eight books, including one written by Lindy, and a major motion picture called *A Cry in the Dark*, starring Meryl Streep. Yet the story remains shrouded in mystery.

To Ferris, one thing is clear. The cause of death was not clearly established, and without that, murder cannot be proved. He was president of the International Association of Forensic Sciences when he was invited by the Chamberlain commission of inquiry to review the case. He flew to Australia to examine the exhibits and study the scientific reports and transcripts. In a four-page preamble to his report, he said the case raised issues about the control of opinion witnesses.

He noted, for example, that without specific training in bloodstain-pattern analysis, a forensic pathologist's opinions "are likely to be determined by what [he] may expect to happen based on his understanding of basic principles and not upon what he knows to happen based on knowledge and experience."

In the report, Ferris questioned whether the stains under the car dashboard were even blood. He noted that the original tests were negative, and that since the trial, evidence had emerged to indicate that the substance was an insulating material applied to the vehicle at the time it was manufactured. He suggested that the sample introduced in court may have been incorrectly labelled. But even if it was blood, he said, the pattern was not typical of the arterial or venous blood spray one would expect if a live baby had its throat slashed. Other stains found in the car, which were positively identified as blood, appeared from their pattern to have been passive droplets from a blood-covered object.

The theory that the bloody marks on the baby's jumpsuit were caused by fingers was not a reasonable conclusion on the basis of the evidence, Ferris wrote. "Similarly, I think it is unreasonable to allow expert opinion based on this 'impression' to construct how a child wearing this clothing may have been held by two hands. It is possible, as with any fabric object, for folding or wrinkling and subsequent contact with a bloodstained surface to produce similar linear marks."

But while he found no evidence to support the Crown's contention that Lindy Chamberlain had killed her baby by slitting her throat, he found no evidence either that the infant had been seized from her bassinet by a dingo. He said the small amounts of blood found in the tent were typical of smears and drops falling passively from a pooled blood source. "There is nothing to indicate they were caused by blood being cast off from the bleeding head of an infant shaken while held in the mouth of an animal." He added that it is unlikely that a dingo's teeth could have plugged the wounds: "The gripping and dragging components of such an injury mechanism would almost certainly have resulted in significant haemorrhage."

Ferris ageed that the forensic evidence supported the conclusion that Azaria's jumpsuit was cut with an implement such as scissors and that her neck was circumferentially wounded. However, he said, without any evidence of active arterial or venous blood spraying, there was no indication that the neck injuries occurred before death. In fact, in his opinion, all of the bloodstains were consistent with post-mortem decapitation.

After the original trial, an appeal court judge ruled that if the stains in the car were blood, then Azaria had been mortally wounded in the car. Ferris said the conclusion pre-sumed that the injuries that caused the blood were the source of death: "[It] does not allow for other theories as to the cause of death not apparently considered at the trial. Is it possible that post-mortem dismemberment of the child's body could have occurred as an attempt to cover up another cause of death such as suffocation — Azaria had apparently been wrapped in five or six layers of blankets so that only the top of her head was exposed — or even crib death?"

There may never be a consensus on how Azaria Chamberlain died. But Ferris would have relished an oppor-tunity to question at the outset the validity of some of the samples and the reconstruction of the crime. Many forensic scientists dread the ordeal of testifying in court, yet Ferris likes what he refers to as "verbal fisticuffs" with lawyers. Many an ill-prepared attorney has withered under an eloquent rebuttal from the now greying but still trim-figured, nattily attired doctor, whose voice and manner are in keeping with his occasional fantasies about another line of work. "My ultimate dream," he once said, "is to be master of an Oxford college, striding through the quadrangles to afternoon tea and sherry, stopping by offices to talk with people, being surrounded by dusty books and thinking — being paid to think. I'm paid to think now but I also have to process paper." To say nothing of bodies.

It is Ferris's ability to clearly explain complex medical evidence to juries that sets him apart in the courtroom. He is, in the words of Larry Cheevers, B.C.'s chief forensic odontologist, a "top gun." "He holds the jury in the tips of his fingers, giving description in minute detail at a level they can understand, without speaking down to them. He's a master." Ferris knows not everyone is as admiring, but he pays scant attention to personal criticism. In a business fraught with fragile egos, he says, "you end up being popular with some people and very unpopular with others."

Ferris's associate, Laurel Gray, who joined the forensic pathology departments at Vancouver General and the University of British Columbia three months after he did, is in some ways his antithesis. Soft-spoken and reticent, she admits that she has sometimes been so nervous before a court appearance or a lecture that she could not sleep or eat. But although she does not exude the same confidence as the male extroverts in her profession, she is certainly as tough-minded. And over the years, she has more than withstood the scrutiny of her peers. "You have to admire her," says Cheevers, "not because she is a woman but because of what she represents as a human being. She is very, very strong — a tremendously stoic human being."

Tall and beautiful with perfectly polished nails, stylish short brown hair and a physique that tells of regular aerobic workouts and holidays spent white-water rafting on the Nahanni River or kayaking around the Queen Charlotte Islands, Gray appears out of place in a morgue surrounded by homicide detectives and corpses. But, like many pathologists, she realized in medical school that she would rather relate to a microscope than talk to a patient.

Gray moved to Vancouver from Toronto in 1981 to do research in lung pathology; ironically, she is a heavy smoker, indulging her habit during working hours in her "second office," a hospital freight elevator that opens onto a parking lot. Her plan was to spend two years in B.C. and then return to Toronto, where her mother, also a pathologist, was director of laboratories at Women's College Hospital and her sisters are practising law and ophthalmology. But Vancouver's spectacular scenery and temperate climate caused her to have second thoughts. Hired by VGH initially for six months, she soon became captivated by the diversity and unpredictability of forensic pathology; a decade later, she is still there.

On weekdays, Gray arrives at her office on the first floor of the Laurel Pavilion at VGH by 7:30 a.m. She and Ferris perform autopsies on alternate days. Outside the morgue, they spend their time attending meetings, lecturing university students in the VGH auditorium or doing paperwork of one sort or another; paperwork accounts for almost half of their jobs. Once a month, on average, they also testify at a major trial and, intermittently, they are called out to the scene of a death. Generally, though, at 8 a.m. every second day, Gray leaves the quiet, clinical atmosphere of her office, lined with books, plants and art, and goes downstairs to the morgue.

Here, the floors are a brick-coloured cement, and the bright lights bounce off the stainless-steel gurneys and wall of crypts. The putrid smell of decomposing corpses frequently wafts through the air, and the loud clanging of another body being delivered goes unnoticed. Gray meets first with the morgue attendants — non-medical staff whose backgrounds vary from hospital porter to criminology graduate and whose jobs include cutting open the bodies and sewing them back up. After they have reviewed the three to four cases that have typically arrived overnight, Gray discusses them with the coroner, either in person or by telephone. Then she establishes a schedule for the day. If there are any homicide cases, the investigating officers are notified so they can unlock the crypt and attend the autopsy. When a corpse is removed from the scene, the police escort the vehicle, watch as the body is placed into the drawer-like compartment, label it, lock it and keep the key to maintain what is called the continuity of evidence. Coroners' cases in which the deaths are not suspicious are stored in white body bags on gurneys in a huge walk-in refrigerator next to the autopsy room.

Ferris says an autopsy for a straightforward homicide case, for example, in which the victim has been shot once in the head, usually takes between one and a half to two hours. That is after the initial external examination, which might itself take up to two hours. If the victim is believed to be HIV-infected, the pathologists wear hard blue plastic masks, which cover their faces, and four pairs of surgical gloves, which, among other things, ensure they work slowly. "It's like defusing a time bomb," he says.

Every couple of days, at least one of the corpses is decomposing. The pathologists again don masks and conduct the autopsy in a small, specially ventilated room outfitted with a powerful fan. Yet they say the putrid smell sticks to their nose hairs for hours. And then there are the maggots, which, even through their gloves, they can feel crawling under their fingers and hear being squashed, their shells crunching like popcorn under their rubber boots.

It is a job that few people, regardless which sex, would be able to handle. Yet after working on many occasions over the past decade with Gray, Larry Cheevers can recall only one instance in which she lost her professional reserve. But, then so did everyone else.

Cheevers and Bart Bastien were working in one corner of the morgue identifying a victim from dental x-rays.

"Laurel and the police were at the autopsy table," says Cheevers, "when, all of a sudden, I heard Laurel say, 'Oh, my God.' But it wasn't just, 'Oh, my God.' It was a cry from the heart. I'll always remember. The whole morgue went silent. We all walked over and looked at the body.

"It was the most horrific brutalization I have ever seen," the dentist recalls. "This guy had bitten the victim in two places and pushed a knife up her vagina. Then he got a steel pipe and rammed it up as well." The pipe had been inserted at least six times, finally tearing through the internal organs into the woman's chest cavity. What Gray had just seen, associated with the passages, was bruising that showed the victim was still alive when it happened. "Laurel was upset. I mean really upset," says Cheevers. "Everyone was. You could just visualize the terrific pain that this woman must have gone through."

When the autopsy was finally over, Gray, Ruth Sellers (a forensic pathologist who attended as an observer), two police officers and Bart Bastien lined up on one side of the morgue while the identification officer on the case took a group photograph. The picture still hangs in a corner of the coroner's office. Gray and Sellers are in their "greens"; the investigating officers are wearing yellow gowns over their uniforms or plain clothes. The clock on the wall behind them reads 8:10; the autopsy began at 3 p.m. The participants have the glazed look of exhaustion that comes not just from working on your feet for five straight hours but from enduring extreme tension for that length of time. But there is also a tangible sense of camaraderie, of the kind of team spirit that emerges when individuals have pulled together and met a formidable challenge.

The bond that forms in those circumstances among diverse professionals — from doctors, dentists and academics to corners, police officers and morgue attendants — is understandable. While each has a different job, all have been stripped of the luxury of innocence. Seeing what no one else sees, and few even want to hear about, they are at one level separated from the rest of the world. One of the ways they cope with the horror is to form a sort of inner circle that often extends beyond work.

In Vancouver, Harley Felstein has traditionally been the person to organize extracurricular activities for the morgue and coroner's staff, from large-scale baseball and golf games followed by the requisite merry-making to smaller, more serious outings such as art-buying trips. "When you are dealing with the type of situation we are, it helps to be able to interact socially," he says. Black humour is another common coping mechanism. Felstein is a funeral director who for more than a decade has run a body-removal service for the coroner's office. He calls it Global Terminal Transportation Services. "I pick up where others drop off," he says. "Never had a client complain."

Felstein's high-energy approach to life is almost a prerequisite among members of the forensic community, whose jobs require them to be on call twenty-four hours a day, 365 days a year. Before he got married a couple of years ago, he was rarely home long enough to cook a meal and existed, he says, almost entirely on deli food. "I suggested he should get rid of his dining-room table," Gray recalls, "because he used it about as much as I use mine." The rest of his apartment in False Creek was taken up with a Jacuzzi and an art collection, including seventeen paintings by his and Gray's favourite artist, Native Canadian Eddy Cobiness.

Felstein's exuberance and enthusiasm over the years have not gone unnoticed by his associates. "He is one of the kindest, most generous people I know," says Ferris. "One of the characters who makes life worth living."

The friendships formed on these outings help to cement the goodwill and co-operative atmosphere on the job. And when members of a team are friends, they tend to take coffee breaks and lunches together and talk about their work, which amplifies the group's synergy. The coffee shop of the Ramada Inn near VGH has long been the "local" of the morgue and coroner's staff. They are on a first-name basis with the servers and have a regular table. Over the years, many a medical mystery has been solved in this setting.

Some homicide cases are so straightforward that they do not require much collaboration. Gray remembers one case, for example, where the perpetrator literally signed his name to the crime. The victim, a fifty-three-year-old man, was found in a hotel room with every inch of his body slashed or beaten, his left ear, eye and nose had been cut off. The killer had carved the initials D. P. on the victim's chest, except the P was backwards. Within a couple of days, the police had arrested a sixteen-year-old dyslexic male with those initials; he was still carrying the razor he had used as the murder weapon.

At another scene Gray attended, a man had been shot during a fight over money. The killer, apparently unaware of the side effects of decomposition or devoid of a sense of smell, simply put the body in the trunk of his car. There it stayed for three months, parked outside the perpetrator's West End home, until neighbours complained to police about flies and putrid fumes.

Most murderers are not so blatant, however. And it seems certain that some of the more devious killers would have gone free without British Columbia's new team approach.

Insobriety is the norm in Vancouver's Skid Row. And so common are unnatural deaths, whether homicides, suicides or accidents, that the derelicts who inhabit its run-down hotels and streets have been known to vacantly step over a corpse without so much as blinking an eye. It is small wonder, then, that for more than twenty years, Paul Jordan chose this festering enclave to seek out sex and drinking partners, typically middle-aged women alcoholics. If they happened to die of alcohol poisoning during the binge, who would be suspicious? Indeed, until 1985, it seems no one was.

In the early eighties, Jordan ran the Slocan Barber Shop at 2503 Kingsway. He had learned his trade in jail. According to newspaper accounts, Jordan was born in Vancouver in 1931, dropped out of school in grade eight, about the time his parents divorced, and embarked on a life of booze and petty crime. The first indication of his predatory nature surfaced in 1961, when he was arrested for allegedly abducting a young Native girl from the Mission Indian Reserve; he was released following a stay of proceedings. Nine months later, he climbed the Lions Gate Bridge during rush hour and threatened to jump off; he was charged with being intoxicated in a public place. The next year, in court on a rape charge, of which he was acquitted, he gave the Nazi salute, threw books at the magistrate and wrestled with police officers. The outburst occurred after the Crown introduced evidence that he was sane and capable of standing trial. A psychiatrist who assessed him at Riverview Mental Hospital concluded that his emotionally immature and impulsive behaviour stemmed from a personality disorder, which rendered him unable to cope with the normal vicissitudes of life.

Jordan was married twice, for three years in the early seventies and for four months in the early eighties. Both wives left him after alleging that he beat them. Shortly after his first marriage, he was found guilty in 1973 of exposing himself to children and of assaulting two women in separate incidents. At a court hearing held to determine whether Jordan was a dangerous sex offender, psychiatrists called by the defence said Jordan's most recent crimes were caused by feelings of sexual inadequacy as he entered middle age. By attacking women, he was trying to "prove his manhood." One of the doctors, Tibor Bezeredi of Vancouver General Hospital, added that there could be no doubt that Jordan was a psychopath and a habitual criminal, but "if he is a dangerous sexual offender, he sure isn't the kind I am used to." Based on the evidence presented to him, which covered only 1973, County Court Judge William Ferry ruled that Jordan did not fit the description of a dangerous offender and, therefore, could not be locked up indefinitely.

By 1983, at least four Native women had died after spending the night with Jordan. The balding barber with thick black glasses even reported some of the deaths himself. But with different detectives, coroners and pathologists working on each case, no one made the connection.

The first hint of foul play came in the fall of 1985. Ferris and Gray had met with the morgue staff early that morning and then headed over to the Ramada with Felstein and Bastien for a quick coffee break. While sipping his usual peppermint tea and eating an English muffin, Ferris told the group about an unusual toxicology report he had received. He had ordered it as a routine follow-up to an autopsy he had performed on a Native woman who had died in Skid Row of alcohol poisoning. Incredibly, it showed a blood-alcohol reading of 790 milligrams percent — almost ten times the legally impaired level and three times the lethal dose for most people. Analysis of the urine and the eye's vitreous fluid had confirmed the result. For that amount of alcohol to be in the woman's body when she died, Ferris figured, she would have had to chugalug twenty-six ounces or more of straight liquor.

Over the previous two years, Gray had performed close to a thousand autopsies. Still, she recalled one six months earlier involving a Native woman from Skid Row, Patricia Thomas, who was subsequently found to have a blood-alcohol reading of 510. A flag went up. Felstein and Bastien, both of whom had been involved in the Vancouver forensic scene longer than Ferris an Gray, started thinking back to cases in which they had been involved. Within a few minutes, they had remembered two.

Viewed alone, each appeared to be either an accidental overdose or a suicide committed by a desperate woman who drank herself to death. When viewed together, the picture was much different. "When you have four deaths occurring in the space of four years in the same place under very similar circumstances with the same phenomenally high alcohol levels," says Gray, "you don't have to be hit over the head to know there is an association."

Sadly, over the next two years, four more women died before Paul Jordan was exposed as the common link and the police had evidence that his involvement was not coincidental. In the absence of the new team approach, however, the fact that the women had been killed might never have been revealed.

Gray attended the four death scenes and did all of the autopsies. Each woman was found in a different Skid Row hotel — Velma Gibbons in the Balmoral in September 1986, Vera Harry in the Clifton two months later, Vanessa Buckner in the Niagara in October 1987 and Edna Shade in the Beacon a month later. All were naked and lying either on the bed or on the floor. By examining their bodies, Gray was able to get some idea of when they died.

Determining how long a person has been dead is not an exact science. However, within a day or so after death, forensic pathologists can usually calculate an approximate time of death by measuring temperature, rigor mortis and lividity. Typically, the body's core temperature drops off at a rate of one degree Fahrenheit an hour, although that can vary widely according to such factors as the weight of the victim, the clothing he is wearing and the external environment. After two hours, rigor mortis starts to set in. It tends to be fully established in eight to twelve hours and begins to dissipate after about twenty-four hours.

About the same time that the muscles begin to stiffen, a purplish discolouration of the skin, known as lividity, starts to show up on the underside of the body. With the heart no longer circulating the blood, it gradually settles, through the natural force of gravity, to the lowest point. After about eight hours, the colour is permanent. Ignorance of this fact has tripped up many a liar. If a body is discovered on its back, for example, with lividity on its front, it is obvious that it has been moved.

By going to each scene, Gray was able to tell that Buckner had been dead the shortest time, three to four hours, and Vera Harry the longest, about eight hours. Back at the morgue, her naked-eye examinations of the victim's organs at autopsy, and her subsequent microscopic assessments of tissue samples, told her that Gibbons, Harry and Shade were all heavy drinkers. Liver cells from the first two showed severe fatty changes and from the latter, the more advanced scarring of cirrhosis. But the tissue samples revealed something much more significant.

In acute high doses, alcohol kills in three ways. First, it depresses the brain, particularly the centres controlling breathing and the beating of the heart, which can simply stop. If the heart and lungs keep working, the alcohol will induce vomiting; if the victim is semi-conscious or unconscious, the vomit will be inhaled into the airways. This can cause death immediately by asphyxiation or slowly as a result of chemical damage to the lungs from stomach acid and concurrent infection and inflammation, known as aspiration pneumonia. As long as the body is alive, it continues to metabolize the alcohol.

Gray learned from the tissue samples that Shade had suffered from pneumonia for about twelve hours before death and Harry, twelve to thirty-six hours; there was no such evidence in Gibbons and Buckner. Assuming that Shade and Harry had nothing to drink for at least twelve hours before they died, Gray expected their toxicology tests to show deceptively low levels of blood-alcohol. They did. Whereas Gibbons's was 630 milligrams percent, Shade's was 100 and Harry's only 40. Through simple arithematic, using an average hourly rate of alcohol metabolism and extrapolating backwards, Gray calculated that Shade and Harry, too, had consumed inordinately high doses.

Long before these final toxicology reports were in, Gray began charting the results of these four and the two autopsies that she and Ferris had conducted in December 1984 and June 1985. All six women had finger-sized bruises on their arms, which, while difficult to interpret, were consistent with being grabbed. Four had bruises on their scalps and two had bruised cheeks or eyes. Was there a serial killer at large using alcohol as a weapon? Gray and Ferris thought so. They asked a local Crown attorney to organize a meeting with the coroners and the police.

After the conference, the authorities searched through twenty years' worth of sudden-death reports, by hand, looking for similar cases. Their efforts paid off. They found that four women had died from alcohol poisoning or aspiration pneumonia between 1965 and 1983 after being with the same person — Gilbert Paul Jordan. Three had died in his barber shop.

When Gray reviewed the early autopsy reports, she found that the women had the same pattern of bruises as the later victims. Still, she says, there was little support for the homicide theory. Yes, the profiles were similar, the police said, but that was exactly the point. It was not uncommon for the inhabitants of Skid Row to drink themselves to death. Furthermore, as the autopsies had documented on the basis of the women's fatty and scarred livers, they had been abusing alcohol for a long time. And alcoholics are prone to bruises.

The toxicology report on Vanessa Buckner would change their minds. Up to then, the highest level of blood-alcohol had been 790; Buckner's was an unthinkable 910. From the onset, though, her case had been different. At twenty-seven years of age, she was younger than most of the other women. She was also black, and was known to abuse drugs but not alcohol. In the Niagara Hotel room in which her body was found, there was a photograph of her newborn infant and a baby's plush toy.

At autopsy, Gray confirmed that Buckner was not a heavy drinker. Unlike every other victim, there was no evidence at all of alcoholism in her liver or other organs. Nor were there any puncture marks in her skin indicative of recent drug use, although, under the microscope, Gray did find the tell-tale signs of chronic intravenous use of oral drugs. Embedded in the lung cells were tiny crystalline particles, remnants of the fillers the drugs had contained.

The fact that Buckner was not a drinker made the blood-alcohol reading of 910 all the more incredible. The concentration in her urine was only half as high, at 440. The disparity told Gray that an enormous amount of alcohol had entered Buckner's body just before she died. In her opinion, it went beyond chugalugging. The liquor must have been literally poured down her throat. In her autopsy report, Gray stated that it would be "extremely unusual for such a level to be obtained by the voluntary ingestion of alcohol." As she later explained in court, "Most people would be unconscious long before that level of alcohol is reached."

Unaware of the damning evidence against him, Jordan set out eleven days after Shade's death, on November 19, 1987, conspicuously well dressed as always, to cruise Skid Row once again. This time, however, he was under police surveillance. When Jordan picked up Rosemary Wilson in a bar and took her to the Balmoral Hotel, officers eavesdropped from the next room. When Wilson began to yell and sounded as though she was gagging, they burst in. The woman later testified that she quickly drank two glasses of straight vodka, which Jordan refused to allow her to mix with juice or 7-Up, saying it was "better for her" that way. Afterwards, she felt as though she was going to pass out, so she sat down on the bed. "He tried to put the bottle down my throat . . . and kill me." Jordan was not detained.

Apparently, the police thought there was still insufficient evidence to support the unusual theory of alcohol as a murder weapon.

Six days later, Jordan was at it again. As Vancouver police sergeant David Jones later told the court, the barber approached nine Native women before he found one willing to accompany him back to the Rainbow Hotel. As the officer listened outside the door, Jordan offered Sheila Joe money to drink up. "I'll give you $50-plus as soon as you finish the drink, I will," Jones heard him say. When the woman said she was only interested in "a little loving," Jordan became belligerent and ordered her to "drink it down, prove it to me. . . . I've been ripped off so many times." At that point, the officer crashed Jordan's party and took the would-be victim to a detoxification centre.

The following day, Jordan was arrested. He was fifty-six years old and living on welfare at the Marble Arch Hotel. Thirty-eight years earlier, he had first appeared in adult court for stealing a car. This time he was accused of first-degree murder in the death of Vanessa Buckner. The charge was later reduced to manslaughter.

At his trial in October 1988, the Crown introduced "similar fact" evidence linking him to the deaths of nine other women, including Shade, Harry and Gibbons. Jordan's lawyer argued that the defendant hadn't meant to kill anyone; he just wanted to have a good time. As far as Gray is concerned, "certainly when there are nine occasions in which your actions have led to a person's death, a reasonable man would be expected to anticipate the same outcome under the same circumstances again."

Jordan was found guilty. In sentencing him to fifteen

years in prison, B.C. Supreme Court Justice John Bouck remarked, "He is a particularly dangerous person since he speaks in a plausible and educated way which masks his true criminal character." In 1991, the B.C. Court of Appeal upheld the conviction but reduced the sentence to nine years.

One aspect of that case that Gray recalls with displeasure are the notes that an inexperienced police officer took in 1984 during the first of the five autopsies she conducted on Jordan's victims. Four years after that initial post-mortem, at Jordan's preliminary hearing, a defence attorney was nearing the end of a lengthy cross-examination of Gray based on her final autopsy reports. The lawyer had started with the last victim and gone backwards in time, finally getting to the case of Patricia Thomas. Suddenly, she turned to Gray and said, seemingly out of the blue, "I believe your conclusion with respect to Thomas was that this death was due to natural causes due to her lifestyle. Do you remember saying that?"

What had happened, Gray says, is that the officer, apparently unaware of the autopsy process, had noted her initial thoughts. Routinely, as she and Ferris go through a case, they talk aloud, using a tape recorder to chronicle their impressions, observations and findings.

"As a pathologist," says Ferris, "you feel very exposed when you have an inexperienced police officer because you don't get any help from them, and they may even misinterpret what you are telling them. As you talk aloud, you are really arguing with yourself and they are writing all this down. You might say, for example, it looks as though this guy has a head injury and the head injury might possibly be the cause of death. You continue to do the autopsy and later you decide, no, he had a heart attack and fell and hit his head. But they will say the head injury is the cause of death. They will also document that he died of a heart attack. It can be very confusing.

"Experienced officers don't put you under any pressure. They don't hover over your shoulder the whole time. They rely on you to show them anything that is relevant.

"It is probably the biggest frustration we have that in a police force the size of Vancouver's, with its own specialist homicide squad, the longest any homicide officer serves at the moment is three years. With the team approach, you can't keep changing the players."

Even when the players remain the same, though, there is a fundamental difference between the way police officers and scientists view their work. The police are trained to rigidly follow regulations; the scientists to question tradition-al concepts. The result can sometimes be an uneasy alliance.

In the early days of Vancouver's evolving team, the police complained that some of the outside experts had no appreciation for the necessity of strict rules governing the collection and storage of exhibits and, in extreme cases, had even independently carted off evidence to their laboratories. Conversely, the forensic pathologists and others complained that the police failed to understand that valuable medical evidence was being lost either because they took too long to do their initial investigations before turning over the remains or they contaminated the body by, for example, spraying it with chemicals to illuminate fingerprints.

Today, many of the smaller issues have been resolved. Yet there are still heady conflicts related to control — both at the scene and throughout the investigation. "If you want to really start an argument," commented one observer, "wait until everyone is together and ask whether the body is an exhibit." As Ferris puts it, "The RCMP has a bit of a siege mentality. When you are under attack, when someone is trying to undermine your authority, you put the wagons in a circle and shoot at anything that moves.

"What they would like is for outside experts to have their own little areas of expertise and leave the collating of the case to the police. My feeling is that the police are not trained to do that job. They need to have forensic experts doing it. Not all police are forensic science experts. I think frequently the police don't understand how the case has to be integrated initially — how a particular piece of evidence may have to be examined by a whole slew of people, which means it may have to be dealt with in a different way."

There will probably always be some tension between the police and the scientists on whose expertise they rely. Beyond all else, they have different agendas. While the police want to nail the perpetrator, the scientists have to remain absolutely impartial, concerned only with deciphering the medical evidence and laboratory findings. Still, as crime-solving becomes increasingly high-tech, the jostling among the disparate members of the partnership is abating through time and education. The emergence of a new breed of police officer with specialized identification training is also helping to bridge the gap between the "old guard" and the scientific experts.

BONES

IN THE INNATELY DELICATE
relationship between the police and outside experts in murder
investigations, Brian Strongman is a rarity. He has a foot in
both camps and is respected by both. The veteran Mountie
has risen through the ranks from identification officer to
inspector. In the early 1980s, he also became the RCMP's
first in-house consultant in forensic anthropology and earned
the admiration not only of his fellow police officers on cases
like the twice-buried body near Ladysmith but of the many
doctors and academics with whom he has worked.

Larry Cheevers, for example, recalls one identification
case that "without Brian's initiative and ingenuity would

never have been solved." The body had been incinerated to the point that the only remains were tiny bone fragments as fragile as tissue paper. Strongman recognized one as a section of jaw bone. By digging a little trench in the ground around it, he managed to transfer it onto a cotton ball and transport it intact to the dentist to be x-rayed. Cheevers had taken one x-ray when the piece fell from his hand to the floor: "I looked down and there was nothing left but ashes. That's all the evidence we had." Fortunately, the x-ray was good and provided enough information to identify the victim from her dental records.

"Brian is a very bright guy," says forensic pathologist James Ferris. "And a real team player."

Part of being a team player is recognizing your limitations, and the scientists admire Strongman for deferring to the experts when the complexity of a case requires it. "I am a firm believer in using fully trained people," Strongman says. "When you have non-scientists doing this type of work, it can lead to problems in court. Once you have a successful challenge to expert evidence in court, it is hard to rescind that black mark. You all of a sudden have case law accepted that can be used in the future against any expert."

The grey-haired but youthful Winnipeg native has a seemingly odd background for his chosen line of work. Before he joined the RCMP in 1964, he studied fine arts at the University of Manitoba for two years. And six years later, when he was posted to Regina, he enrolled in night school, taking up sculpture, among other things.

In 1986, Strongman was promoted to the rank of inspector and spent several years on the RCMP's administrative side as the staffing officer for the province of Alberta. He is now back where he likes it best, in operations, second-in-command of twenty-one detachments in the region of Nelson, B.C. And he could not be happier with the location. Looking out the window of his office down the waters of Kootenay Lake to his current favourite hiking spot, he says, "This has to be the most beautiful spot in the world."

Strongman was just twenty when he joined the RCMP and embarked on the six months of boot camp that all recruits have endured for more than a century. Basic training was followed by the usual whirlwind of transfers designed to test the mettle of young members. In six years, he was posted to nine detachments in British Columbia, Alberta and the Arctic. But rather than becoming a jack-of-all trades within the force, he was gradually learning everything there was to know about identification.

As Strongman had anticipated, his arts training has been a boon to him both on and off the job. Many a family vacation has been spent hiking and skiing through the mountains of western Canada, with Strongman capturing the scenery first on film and, back at home, in watercolour paintings. Part of the reason he pursued an education in fine arts was his love of photography, which he took up as a hobby when he was a teenager. But unlike many creative types, he also enjoys the analytical side of things. He applied to become an RCMP identification officer because he realized it would satisfy both interests and allow him to spend most of his time out on the road, away from a desk.

At his first posting in Nanaimo, Strongman offered to work on his off-time in the darkroom, developing film taken by the identification team at crime scenes. Eventually, he was invited to accompany the team and from then on, he says, he was "bumped from pillar to post gaining experience on the job from the experienced members." He landed two temporary jobs as a junior ident officer in Vancouver and New Westminster before drawing two months of formal training in Ottawa in 1967 and his first permanent ident position in Kamloops.

Over the years, Strongman's love of things analytical flourished. In 1979, he was promoted to the rank of sergeant and placed in charge of the identification unit at the Coquitlam detachment outside Vancouver. He had been there a couple of years when his office was notified of a special course in forensic anthropology being offered at Simon Fraser University in nearby Burnaby. For more than a century, physical anthropologists have been identifying skeletal remains of forensic significance in their university or museum laboratories. However, their status as forensic scientists and their presence at crime scenes is relatively recent.

Strongman was intrigued by the science. As he well knew by then, bodies rarely turn up as complete skeletons. Instead, ravaged by violence, fire, animals or simply the elements, they are more likely to consist of hundreds, or even thousands, of tiny bone fragments, or maybe just a skull without dental work or even teeth. He found it fascinating that a forensic anthropologist could, from such scant evidence, distinguish between human and animal bones, determine whether the bones belonged to only one person, and then often derive clues about that person's sex, age, race, height and even the manner of death. He didn't hesitate for a second before signing up.

"We have many set means of identification, but if you have a body that is skeletal with no fingerprints and no dental work, where do you go from there? So I started taking these courses to see if I could expand my identification methods."

The course instructor was Mark Skinner, a professor of physical anthropology, whose passion for forensic work dates to his childhood in Medicine Hat, Alberta, where his father, a physician and coroner, occasionally allowed him to tag along on cases. Skinner impressed Strongman as a "really nice guy — quiet, unassuming and very intelligent." As a teacher, "he went out of his way to help anyone who showed an interest in the subject, and he always treated me as a peer." And as a forensic scientist, "he was an expert in his field and had a real eye for investigation." The two soon became good friends.

One of the first class assignments was a paper on the use of probability studies in identification. "You will be interested in this," Skinner told Strongman, handing him a human skull without the lower jaw. The artifact had been discovered in 1977 beside a stream in Port Coquitlam and, after hanging around the coroner's office for several years without being identified, had been turned over to the university.

The missing mandible would have made it easier to determine the person's race and sex. The lower jaw in a female is typically smaller and lighter than a male's and usually shows a uniform graceful curve; as well, a man's jaw is normally flat opposite the four incisor teeth. To further complicate matters, there were no upper teeth in the skull. Nonetheless, Strongman concluded from a large body of research on the topic that the steepness of the forehead and the large supraorbital ridges above the eyes, among other things, showed the skull belonged to a man.

When he measured the height and width of the skull, adding in an average-sized jaw, he found it was long and narrow as is typical of Caucasians. There were also angular orbital openings, as opposed to the rectangular openings common in Afro North Americans and the rounded openings usual in East Asians and North American Natives.

Finally, he examined the sutures between the skull bones. On the interior, they were all totally fused and had tiny pit marks on each side of the closing, which is indicative of advanced age. Strongman estimated the age at sixty-seven to seventy-seven or, expressed another way, seventy-two plus or minus five years.

Without the limb bones, he could draw no conclusions about the person's height. And there were no apparent signs of violence. The only distinguishing feature was a deviated septum, which could have meant the person inherited a crooked nose or had broken it at some point in his life.

Armed with this profile, and knowledge of where the skull had been found, Strongman went back to his office to pore over the missing-person files. His search turned up one promising lead. Three years before the skull was found, a seventy-two-year-old man had been reported missing from a senior citizens' home ten blocks from the stream where the skull was discovered. The man had never been found.

On the basis of statistical probability alone, Strongman says, he could not conclude that the skull belonged to the missing man. However, he obtained a photograph of the senior that, even at first glance, left little doubt: the man's nose was decidedly twisted to the right. When Strongman then superimposed images of the photograph and the skull on a single screen, he knew he had an exact match. The shape of the head, the cheek-bones, the eyesockets and the nasal cavities all lined up perfectly. The coroner's court agreed and the case was finally closed.

The next step for Strongman was learning to physically put a face on a skull through a process known as facial reconstruction. Here his training in sculpture gave him a head start. Consulting charts of known standards for tissue depths, which vary according to age, race and sex, he was able to take plastic casts of actual skulls and use Plasticine to slowly build up the soft tissue, muscle by muscle. For the noses, ears and lips, for which there are no standards, he relied on artistic licence.

Over the next year, Strongman moved from the classroom into the field. In the woods of Burnaby Mountain, not far from the university campus, Skinner buried the carcasses of large game animals to teach his students how to recognize the typically depressed area of ground that indicates a burial site and then how to carefully retrieve the remains. The exercise also allowed them to study the rate of decomposition in wet soil; the moisture, temperature and composition of the ground in which a body is buried all affect how fast it decays, which in turn affects the estimate of elapsed time since death. In a very dry environment, a body tends to mummify; in hot, wet surroundings, it quickly rots.

The archaeological techniques used in retrieving skeletal remains have long been applied to the unearthing of ancient civilizations, but their value in forensic cases had just begun to be appreciated in Canada in 1983. That year, the RCMP asked Strongman to deliver a series of lectures on forensic anthropology as part of the advanced identification course offered at the Canadian Police College in Ottawa.

In January 1984, Strongman received a phone call from the Mountie in charge of the identification unit at the Nanaimo detachment on Vancouver Island. He had attended one of those talks. That morning, the officer told Strongman, two plain-clothes members of the General Investigative Services had hauled a large drum-like screen into his office and asked him where they could sterilize it.

"What do you want to do that for?" the ident chief had asked.

"Well, there's this firepit we want to sift through to see if we can find any remains."

"Whoa, wait a minute. There are people who might be able to help you."

Although forensic anthropologists specialize in identifying skeletal human remains, as Strongman had learned early on from Skinner and in turn had emphasized to his audience at the police college, the context in which the remains are recovered is critical. In excavations, for example, if anthropologists don't control for time — that is, determine what went down first — and preserve the physical relationships between objects, the evidence can be misleading or even meaningless.

"For example," Skinner used to say, "if a victim was blindfolded and you don't excavate the remains carefully, you might not be able to tell whether he was wearing a bandanna, a blindfold or a neckerchief. Or a bullet that was just sitting in some guy's pocket could fall through his decomposing body."

The Nanaimo Mountie knew that if the incinerated debris was treated as a mini-archaeological dig, the homicide investigators had a much better chance of uncovering useful information. It is unlikely, however, that he could have dreamed just how much evidence would be revealed because of his intervention.

Before she disappeared on Friday, December 16, 1983, Lisa Clark worked as a nurse's aid at Trillium Lodge, a senior citizens' home in Parksville, B.C. A cheerful, popular twenty-year-old with long brown hair and a ready smile, she usually spent her free time at her grandparents' twenty-eight-hectare farm in Cedar Valley, just south of Nanaimo. Two months earlier, at a Nanaimo cabaret, Lisa had met Guy McInnes, a twenty-one-year-old trade school student. Since then, she had spent more and more time at the rural cabin McInnes rented with Kevin Arkell, a nineteen-year-old grade-school dropout.

On Thursday night, Lisa and McInnes attended a fashion show at which her older sister was one of the models. Afterwards, they went to a couple of nightclubs and then returned to his cabin on the western edge of town. There they smoked a joint and sat talking with Arkell.

At one point, Lisa asked the two men if they wanted to see what a $1,000 bill looked like. Two weeks earlier, she had been in a car accident. She was slightly injured and her car was written off. As a result, she had just received an insurance settlement of $1,400. She had the money with her, she explained, because the next day she was planning to take a Datsun she had seen at a Nanaimo dealership out for a test drive.

Before they went to bed, McInnes arranged for Arkell, who liked to work on cars and consequently knew a lot about them, to take Lisa to the car lot. When he left for school that Friday morning, he said later, his girlfriend and roommate were still sleeping.

Shortly after 11 a.m., Lisa and Arkell arrived at the dealership and took the Datsun out for about an hour. On their return, Lisa told the salesman she had decided to buy the vehicle; she wanted to put $1,100 down and finance the rest through the credit union. When she was unable to reach the loans officer, she left with Arkell. She was wearing a new zippered rabbit-fur bomber jacket, pearl earrings, a wrist watch and a ring.

About 1 p.m., Arkell's father happened to see his son driving along the highway towards the cabin in his red Trans Am with a young dark-haired woman. He noticed they were laughing and appeared to be having a good time. The next day, Saturday, his son came to his home to borrow a shovel.

Lisa had arranged to meet McInnes after his classes on Friday afternoon. When she did not show up, he was not worried; he assumed that she was out with her friends. But when she failed to report for work Saturday morning, her employer called her father, who notified the RCMP.

Early the next week, McInnes noticed embers in a firepit behind a ramshackle chicken coop at the rear of the cabin. He didn't give it a second thought, he said later: "I just thought Kevin was cleaning up the yard."

Three weeks later, Donald Grais, a small-time marijuana dealer, read a story about Lisa's disappearance in the Nanaimo *Times*; the article mentioned a $1,000 bill. Grais had given Arkell change for one the weekend Lisa went missing. He called the police and made an appointment to talk to them in the morning.

That same night, Arkell showed up at Grais's apartment. The drug dealer showed Arkell the newspaper article, remarking, "There's not too many $1,000 bills around Nanaimo." At first, Arkell denied knowing anything about it. When Grais pushed the issue, he finally said he had stolen it from Lisa's purse while she slept.

Arkell stayed at Grais's home that night and was still asleep when Grais left for his meeting with the police. On his return, Grais questioned Arkell further.

"Finally, he told me what happened," he later testified. "He said they were up at the cabin and in the morning they went in to a car lot and test-drove a car. They went back to the cabin, and as they were leaving, she was walking in front.

"She just suddenly started gasping and choking and he grabbed her but her body went limp and lifeless and she just fell.

"He freaked out and didn't know what to do. He said he was going to bury her but he put her under a blanket or something and hid her.

"He thought they'd find her if he buried her, so he went out to Canadian Tire and got some gas and old tires. . . . He said he lit her and burned her to a cinder."

Arkell was charged with first-degree murder. While at Wilkinson Road Prison awaiting trial, he allegedly told a fellow inmate another story. He said he had taken Lisa back to the cabin on the pretence that McInnes wanted to meet her there. Once there, he tried to sexually assault her, but she managed to break free and run outside. He said he ran her down with his car and then smashed her in the head with a large rock.

It was 10 a.m. on January 12, 1984, when Strongman got the call from the Mountie in Nanaimo. He immediately called Simon Fraser University to see if Skinner could also go to the scene. Although Strongman had taken forensic anthropology courses part-time for five years by then, he knew this case required an expert. Skinner had been assisting the police in British Columbia on homicide cases since 1976. And in 1982, he had achieved formal accreditation as a forensic anthropologist by writing board examinations set by the American Academy of Forensic Sciences.

After arranging to meet Skinner at the scene the next morning, Strongman flew to Vancouver Island by helicopter. The chopper landed in a clearing in heavy bush off the Jingle Pot Road. Several police investigators and forensic pathologist Sheila Carlisle were gathered around a large burn pile near the chicken coop behind McInnes's cabin.

To the untrained eye, it would have seemed hopeless even to try to uncover anything meaningful in the heap of incinerated debris. The remnants of steel-belted radial tires, wooden timbers, tin cans, springs from a sofa and, as it turned out, animal bones were strewn among the ashes. To Strongman, though, the scene presented an interesting challenge. He looked at it analytically and said simply, "This sort of scene has to be systematically taken apart from the surface down."

The other Mounties at the scene had no experience in forensic anthropology. Initially, Strongman recalls, there was a palpable, although unspoken, sense of impatience with the excruciatingly slow pace. In preparation for Skinner's arrival, Strongman got the Nanaimo identification officers to build an eight-foot square out of two-by-fours and convert it into a grid by rigging it with nails and strings to create 256 six-inch squares. The grid was then placed over the firepit and photographed from above with a four-by-five camera by one of the officers who crawled along an extension ladder suspended over the pit by step-ladders. The same officer had previously taken ground and aerial shots of the entire scene.

Meanwhile, Strongman sketched the contents of each square. Although the sky was clear and the ground bare, it was bitterly cold. By the day's end, long ice crystals had formed on his sketch pad. Nonetheless, from the time Skinner arrived the next morning, it took the team just two ten-hour days — working under portable lights after dark — to recover the fragile evidence that would ultimately convict Arkell.

Kneeling at the edge of the grid, surrounded by dust-pans, brushes, trowels and other archaeological tools, Skinner, Strongman and Carlisle, who remained at the scene in case any tissue was uncovered, worked together to recover, layer by layer, the contents of each square. Each exhibit was identified, packaged and given a number that was cross-referenced to its grid location. The entire process was further recorded by videotape.

Among the first exhibits retrieved from the ashes were the bone fragments that the initial investigating officers had intended to retrieve with the drum-shaped screen. When Skinner identified them as animal bones, they were crestfall-en. Their disappointment disappeared, however, when the first human fragments were unearthed.

Because of his training and experience, Skinner was able to identify each tiny piece of bone as it was uncovered; as he did, Strongman noted it on his paper grid. Eventually, a rough outline emerged of the position in which the body had been placed on the fire: face down with the left arm out to the side, the left knee bent upwards, and the right arm resting against her pelvis.

Skinner further determined from the condition of the bones that the heat in the pit had reached 870 to 980 degrees Celsius, comparable to that generated in a crematorium and sufficient to reduce human bone to powder. Indeed, Strongman says, "Some pieces of skull were so fragile they were almost like tissue paper. If they had gone through the drum screen . . ."

Various charred artifacts, including a metal keychain with the name Lisa on it and a woman's diamond watch with the hands welded by heat to the time 3:20, were also discovered at the scene. Smaller personal effects, among them a ring and the post from a pearl earring, were sifted from the ashes later.

"By the end," says Strongman, "all that was left was sand and dirt with nothing obvious in it. But we scooped all that out too and packaged and labeled it, until we hit solid bed dirt."

When Skinner analyzed the exhibits back in his laboratory, he confirmed the position of the body and determined, from the location of several fire-resistant bits of clothing, including a jacket zipper and brassiere hoops, that it had been fully clothed when it was set ablaze.

Even more incredible was that he was able to rebuild portions of the skull by piecing together more than a hundred fragments uncovered in the ashes. And when he was finished, there was clear evidence that a sharp instrument like an axe had been driven into the head at least four times. One of the cut marks was on the inside of a piece of the back of the skull. That told Skinner the weapon had gone right through the brain. He noted, too, that the edges of the weapon marks had melted, which meant they had been inflicted before the body was placed on the fire. Skinner found nothing in his analysis to corroborate Arkell's story that the victim had been hit on the head with a large rock.

The murder weapon was still missing when the case went to trial that fall, so to illustrate his findings, Skinner had painted sections of a plastic skull blue to correspond to the portions he had been able to reconstruct. He coloured the cut marks yellow. The top of the model opened like a lid to allow the jury to view the interior. Using it, as well as photograph blow-ups of the actual wound marks, he explained to the court how he was able to conclude, as had Ferris, that the murder weapon was probably a hatchet.

What happened next, Strongman says, was right out of a Perry Mason show. "It was a Friday afternoon and Mark Skinner had just given his evidence when this friend of the accused who was in the courtroom says to the guy sitting next to him, 'Geez, I lent him my axe.' He was also sitting beside one of our investigators."

As it turned out, the friend had unwittingly retrieved his metre-long woodsman's axe from the cabin before Arkell was arrested. The RCMP picked up the tool and took it to Staff Sgt. Don Watson in the Vancouver forensic laboratory; Watson worked non-stop that weekend comparing the blade with the cuts in the victim's skull. When he found that a burr on one side of the blade matched a notch in the wound marks, he told the jury, "I came to the conclusion that this axe, and no other axe, made the pattern found on the skull bone."

Arkell was sentenced to twenty-five years in prison on the strength of the physical evidence.

For Skinner, it was the second case of its kind. In 1976, the RCMP were contacted by a woman who said that five years previously she had helped burn and bury the body of her boyfriend. He had been killed, she alleged, by another man in a remote area of the West Coast. Skinner located the burial site and recovered more than ten thousand pieces of bone, most of which were less than six millimetres in size. Here, too, he had exercised the same caution and techniques that an archaeologist in Egypt might use to unearth the remains of an ancient pharaoh. This case took much longer, however; he and the investigating team spent nine hundred man-hours working at the scene alone.

The remains were concentrated in an area just over a metre square. After carefully stripping back the moss, they covered the site with a grid comprised of fifteen-centimetre squares. Each layer of earth in each square was sifted, and its contents were packaged and labelled. Later, after Skinner identified the bone chips, he recorded where they were recovered on a map using the same grid, revealing the victim's position. By distinguishing between bones from the right and left side of the body, he determined that the body had been lying on its back. Furthermore, by estimating the temperature to which each side of the individual bone fragments had been exposed — as it heats, bone changes colour from white to brown to black to blue-grey to white again and then begins to distort, crack and bend — he concluded that the fire had been built on top of the body. His findings confirmed the woman's account of the crime.

In spite of the significant contribution that forensic

anthropologists can make to such crime-scene investigations, their discipline is still very much in the pioneering stages in Canada. Part of the reason, Skinner believes, is that there are only a handful of physical anthropologists across the country who promote their potential value at death scenes, and they are university or museum-based. By practising "outside traditional bureaucracies which deal with found human remains, they can quickly be forgotten." But their image problem extends to the general public and even their own profession. "One's colleagues may question whether such work is truly scholarly," he wrote in an article published in 1989 in the *Canadian Society of Forensic Science Journal*, "and similarly the public considers professorial types too theoretical to be useful."

It is a situation that applies equally to another newcomer to death-scene investigations in Canada: the forensic entomologist.

MAGGOTS AS CLOCKS

J OHN BORDEN AND AKBAR
Syed were initiated into the world of homicide investigations
in 1985. The entomologists, or insect specialists, were working in their labs at Simon Fraser University when fellow
professor Mark Skinner called from a murder scene near
Kootenay, B.C. If he brought them the maggots from the
decomposing corpse, Skinner asked, could they rear them
to estimate the elapsed time since death? Bring them in,
Syed said.

Once a body has been dead for more than seventy-two
hours and has started to decay, it is difficult for pathologists
to pin down the time of death. Bodies decompose at vastly

different rates depending on a variety of factors ranging from their size to the weather. Insects, however, are always drawn to a body in the same order, whether it is dumped in a field or stashed in an attic.

Flies arrive first — within twenty-four hours during spring, summer and fall, and within minutes if blood or other bodily fluids are present. These include the family *Muscidae*, commonly called houseflies, and the sightly larger, often metallic blue or green *Calliphoridae*, or blowflies. They lay batches of eggs in wounds or in natural orifices. The eggs hatch, after a set period, into masses of whitish, two-millimetre-long maggots.

The larvae go through three distinct phases while feeding on the body, finally wandering away from the corpse to pupate in clothing or in the soil. Burrowing into a safe place, they loosen themselves from their outer shells, and the shells harden and darken to a deep brown within a few hours. After a certain number of days, an adult fly emerges from the protective covering and the cycle starts again. The presence of empty pupal cases indicates to an entomologist that at least one generation of flies of this species has developed on the corpse.

Grey-checked fleshflies, or *Sarcophagidae*, are among the second wave of insects. Once the body fats turn rancid and the tissues ferment, larder beetles, cheese-skippers, lesser houseflies and hover-flies come. Later, there are carrion beetles, then certain species of mites, followed by another type of carrion beetle.

By knowing the succession of insects that invade a dead body and the life span of each, entomologists can often give a rough estimate of death immediately. Then, by collecting the larvae and pupae and raising them in their laboratories, they can refine their calculations. They can also tell that the body has been moved if there are insects that are not indigenous to the location in which it was found.

The first use of bugs in murder investigations is said to date back to thirteenth-century China. As legend has it, a farmer was killed by blows from a sickle on a hot summer day. The authorities gathered together all the farmers in the area and told them to lay their sickles on the ground. When blowflies landed on only one of the tools, its owner confessed. References to forensic entomology in the Western world are more recent. In 1850, in the town of Arbois in France, a plasterer repairing a mantelpiece is reported to have discovered a baby's body. The occupants of the house were the obvious suspects until a naturalist determined that the tiny corpse had been attacked by insects for two years, implicating the previous tenants.

In 1894, French scientist J. P. Megnin stated, in a now classic paper entitled "La Faune des Cadavres," that a body left in open air is invaded in succession, at predictable stages, by eight types of insects. By identifying the bugs, he said, one could estimate the time of death.

After Borden and Syed were able to provide the police with an estimated time of death based on the maggots they received from Skinner, insects collected from decomposing bodies regularly began arriving at their laboratory. On their seventh case, the scientists were called to the actual scene.

It was nine days before Christmas 1986. A man had gone looking for a Christmas tree in an isolated stretch of woods off an old logging road at the foot of Mount Seymour in North Vancouver. What he found was not at all in keeping with the yuletide spirit: the decomposing body of one woman and the skeletal remains of another, both extensively gnawed by animals.

As the sun shone brightly, filtering through the sixty-metre trees of the West Coast forest, Borden, Syed and four other scientists, all in blue coveralls, knelt side by side on the frosty ground, each bent to their separate tasks. The entomologists, wearing face masks to protect them from swarming flies and the stench of rotting flesh, crouched beside the fresher body, digging out larvae. At the same time, a botanist gingerly removed plant material and soil samples that would help him assess how long the bodies had been lying at that site. A physical anthropologist and his assistant, surrounded by archaeological tools, painstakingly collected the skeletal remains and recorded their precise location. And forensic pathologist James Ferris searched the gruesome arena for information that might tell him not only whether the women had died there or been dumped there after their deaths but also the precise nature of their injuries and how they had been killed.

Working alongside the scientists, RCMP identification officers looked for fingerprints and bloodstains, took videotapes and still photographs, and carefully packaged and documented each exhibit. Police divers scoured the bottom of a nearby creek, and Mounties with dogs combed the surrounding woods. The fastidious exercise lasted six hours.

Syed commented afterwards that the co-operative atmosphere made the ordeal bearable: "If there had just been one or two of us, it would have been scary. But with so many of us working together, it was okay." Even though he and Borden had been wearing gloves, they had trouble getting rid of the smell on their hands.

Back at the university insectary, Syed killed the adult beetles and some of the adult flies they had collected and pinned them for identification; he put other adult flies in a small cage with water and sugar. He mounted the mites found on the beetles on slides. He washed the maggots to remove the soil and placed them on a fresh piece of beef liver on sawdust in a glass jar so they could complete their larval development and pupate. Those that had already pupated were kept separately in Petri dishes where he could record the emergence of the adults. Finally, he sent specimens of the adult insects to the Bio-Systematics Research Institute in Ottawa for positive identification.

At the scene, Borden and Syed had provided the police and Ferris with a rough two-month estimate of the time of death of the fresher body. A week or so later, after studying the insects in the laboratory, they were able to refine their estimate to a one-week period.

Although this case remains unsolved, the entomologists' participation in the crime-scene team increased awareness of the significant contribution they could make to homicide investigations. Thereafter, the demand for their services snowballed. By late 1987, it had evolved into essentially a part-time job, which Borden, as head of the department of biological sciences, and Syed, as supervisor of the insectary, were too busy to take on. Borden offered it to Gail Anderson, a twenty-five-year-old graduate student and native of Cleveland, England.

At first, Anderson was not sure if she could handle it. She had completed a master's degree in pest management and was working on a PhD in entomology. But she had never seen a dead body, apart from one preserved anatomy cadaver at the University of Manchester, where she did her undergraduate degree in zoology — and that was from a distance. Borden, though, "saw a future in it," she says, "and he is very convincing."

Ultimately, Anderson's passion for entomology prompted her to accept. "I wanted to study insects in a way that would be beneficial — for disease prevention, say, or as biological pest controls. I thought, this has to be one of the most practical applications. I had no idea how it was going to be. I said, 'I'll give it a year and we'll see . . .'"

It was on a Saturday of a holiday weekend in the summer of 1988 that Anderson got her first case. She was not called to the scene. She met RCMP Cpl. Bob Stair, an identification specialist, at her lab, where he turned over more than a dozen vials containing adult beetles and different sizes of maggots, collected from various parts of the body and the immediate area. A quick look told Anderson she probably had everything she needed, but since it was her first case, she wanted to be absolutely certain.

"Were there any more of the larger-sized maggots?" Anderson asked the Mountie.

"Lots," he said. "I can get more for you after the autopsy on Tuesday."

Anderson said she would like to collect the larvae herself.

"Have you ever seen a decomposing body?" Stair asked.

"No, I haven't," Anderson replied bluntly. "In the normal course of life, one doesn't."

In her lab, it took Anderson all afternoon and evening

to deal with the evidence that Stair had collected. The insects from each vial had to be kept separately. The young scientist dealt first with the maggots; they have to be kept alive so they can be identified by species when they develop into adult flies. Each species has a different life span, and there currently is no easy way to tell them apart before they are fully developed. The adult insects would be killed and pinned to a chart with labels later.

Anderson took the vials of larvae into one of a dozen environmentally controlled cubicles next door to her laboratory. From the wooden shelves lining the room, she took down large clear bottles resembling cookie jars. In the bottom of each jar she poured a layer of sawdust. Next, she put in a sheet of brown paper towel, folded and sightly dampened. On top of the paper, she placed a fresh slab of beef liver about the size of a man's fist. Then she gently paced the maggots on top of the meat and covered the opening with a sheet of paper towel secured with an elastic band; that would allow the larvae to breathe but not escape. Finally, she labelled each jar with its myriad identifying numbers.

Before leaving the room, she set the temperature to that of the crime scene, the lights to mimic the current hours of daylight, and locked the door. She would check the insects every day. As soon as the larvae burrowed into the sawdust and pupated, she would transfer them to a Petri dish to await their emergence as adult insects.

It was not a pleasant exercise: "The insects come out smelling horrible. The liquid from the decomposed body tissues and the soil smells. You are working in a small enclosed space and your imagination runs wild. You picture things much worse than they are."

Ironically, that made Anderson's trip to the morgue on Tuesday easier than she had anticipated. When she arrived, she expected that the autopsy would be finished, but Laurel Gray was just beginning. Beside Laurel was another familiar face, Bart Bastien. Steeling herself, Anderson went in. "It was not as bad as I thought. It smelled unpleasant but it wasn't as macabre as I had expected. My attention was immediately taken over by the insects and what they were likely to tell me or not to tell me. It would be horrifying if you were just an observer, if you came across this sort of thing in the bush. But to be there for a purpose — to stop this from happening again — it's not that bad."

The assistant entomology professor says even some fellow insect specialists who spend their days scrutinizing bugs in every stage of development have asked her how she can stomach her job. She explains simply that she focuses only on the larvae or pupae and on what they can tell her. Everything else she blanks out. Like most forensic scientists, she says it is easier if she does not know any personal details. On a similar note, she says she would probably find it more disturbing to work on a fresh body because it looks like a human being.

Anderson would prefer to be called to more scenes than she is, as she makes abundantly clear in a handout she has written for her training course for police officers: "The first and most important stage of the procedure involved in forensic entomology involves careful and accurate collection of insect evidence at the scene. This involves knowledge of the insects' behaviour, therefore it is best performed by an entomologist. Unfortunately, the entomologist is not usually called until after the body has been removed from the death scene. I usually see the remains at the morgue, and in some cases, do not actually see the remains at all, so my evidence is dependent on accurate collection by the investigating officers."

In determining the time of death, Anderson must also consider how external influences may have accelerated or inhibited the usual time period for the development of each insect. These range from the weather to the amount of soil that might have been covering the victim.

Crime-scene investigators who have taken her course now routinely provide her with videos, photographs and written descriptions of the scene and the body, in addition to the insect evidence. She has explained that although the major groups of insects are always drawn to a body in the same order, different species may be present, for example, in a house, by a roadside, in the woods or on a beach; that maggots may move farther away from the body if the soil has good drainage or if they can't find a suitable place to pupate close to the body; that the victim's clothing may limit or facilitate the attack; and that cooler-than-normal temperatures, which might be expected at high elevations or in the shade, may slow down the insects' development. Whenever possible, Anderson tells them, it is a good idea to record the temperatures at outdoor scenes for a week or more, so they can be compared with the official temperatures at the nearest weather station. Since those official temperatures are used in calculating the life span of the insects, a significant variation could lead to a misinterpretation of the data.

As part of her teaching courses, Anderson also sets out twenty-kilogram carcasses of young pigs, roughly the same size as a man's torso, in the woods north of the Fraser River.

Her students visit these every two days to see how waves of insects attack a body in various settings. The exercise also allows Anderson to document which insects invade the animals at what times during different seasons and under various conditions. She has found, for example, that although the insects in B.C. arrive in the same order as in other parts of Canada, many arrive sooner.

Anderson lives on two hectares of land in the Fraser Valley near Langley with her husband, Gregory, and myriad pets, including horses, chinchillas and a tiny African pygmy hedgehog. Although she has precious little time to spend at home, especially in the summer months, she says she is happy with her job: "I get to do the research and to enjoy a totally different side of university life — going out and applying the science in a very practical way. You couldn't be in my position and do just one: you need to do the research to back up the field work; you need to do the field work to know what to research."

When she started, she says she was concerned not only about how she would react to decomposing bodies but also about how the police and other crime-scene investigators, most of whom are middle-aged men, would react to her. "I was worried that because I was young and female they wouldn't listen to me." With her short dark hair and the jeans and sneakers she sometimes wears in her laboratory, Anderson still looks very much the university co-ed.

Happily, she says, in the seven years that she has now been working with and training police officers and others, she has never detected even a hint of chauvinism — "no suggestion from anyone that they didn't completely envelop my ideas." She attributes that in part to her enthusiastic attitude towards her work and to her ability to explain it well: "I'm a teacher now — a university prof." An observer might wonder if it isn't her matter-of-fact approach to what by any standards is often extremely gruesome work. "The police are very keen," she adds. "Every cop who has been on the beat for any length of time has seen decomposed remains with bugs." If they cannot pin down the time of death, the investigation is much more difficult: for one thing, alibis cannot be rejected.

In 1935, in Edinburgh, Scotland, a doctor who went to great lengths to conceal the murder of his allegedly unfaithful wife and the family's nursemaid — to the point of excising their identifying features and tossing them into a stream — was convicted after a scientist determined the time of death by examining maggots on the bodies, discrediting the doctor's story.

While homicide investigators in Europe have relied on insect evidence for a full century, detectives in North America viewed bugs as nothing more than an unpleasant nuisance until ten or fifteen years ago. And even now, Anderson says, only a handful of entomologists across the entire continent are actively involved in forensic work; coincidentally, the only other Canadian is also a woman, Dael Morris at the Royal Ontario Museum in Toronto.

Part of the reason for their low profile may be that they seldom have to attend court. Their information is most important to sudden-death investigations at the onset, helping the police in murder cases, for example, to narrow down the suspects by confirming or discounting their alibis.

Anderson had been on the job for nearly six years before she was called to testify for the first time, in

December 1993. Initially, the case was strangely reminiscent of Borden and Akbar's first murder scene. On May 17, 1992, a man looking for firewood near a remote logging road northwest of Courtenay on Vancouver Island discovered a body. "All I saw was one hand with rings on it lying on a bank and I took off and went to the police. . . . It was pretty ugly," John Barnside, a sawmill employee, told newspaper reporters.

When the police arrived, they discovered the bodies of two fully clothed women. Both had been shot in the head. One of the officers at the scene had taken Anderson's course and knew how to collect the insect evidence — picking up delicate specimens with an artist's brush dipped in water, and packaging them in vials with tiny air holes blocked with cheesecloth so they would stay alive. Maggots, he knew, had to have food in their containers. Equally important, they could not be mixed up, since beetle larvae, for example, feed on fly larvae.

Midafternoon on May 20, Sgt. Dennis Colburn of the RCMP's Comox air section arrived at Anderson's lab with sixteen vials of what the scientist later identified as *Coleoptera* adults and *Diptera* eggs, larvae, pupae and adults. The adult insects were pinned. Most of the immature species were raised to adulthood in a secured cubicle in the insectary; some were preserved in alcohol.

Anderson kept notes on the insects' development until June 17, almost a month. She calculated from this information, and from Environment Canada weather records for the Courtenay area, that both women died at the same time and that "death must have occurred on or before 8 May, and most probably occurred on or before 6 May."

The police, in the meantime, had arrested two suspects near Smithers, in northwestern B.C. James Andrew Doherty, twenty-seven, and Lex Arthur Primeau, thirty-one, both of Campbell River, were charged with murder in connection with the shooting deaths. Doherty was kept in custody; Primeau was released on bail. Six months later, Primeau died after a lone gunman fired shots through the living-room window of his house in Campbell River.

At Doherty's Supreme Court trial in Nanaimo in November 1993, two men testified that they saw the accused shoot the women in the early morning hours of May 3, 1992. And a firearms expert said that cartridges found at the scene and later in Doherty's car and truck appeared to have been fired from the same gun. However, three defence witnesses said they saw one of the victims alive after May 3. The first said she saw the woman on May 6; the other two said the woman was one of four people in a turquoise GMC camper truck that drove slowly by them on May 9 as they were leaving a shopping centre parking lot.

Midway through the trial, Mr. Justice Ralph Hutchinson ruled that forensic pathologist Kerry Pringle was not qualified to testify about when the two victims died. Before the ruling, Pringle had candidly told the court that he believed, like most forensic pathologists, that "estimating the time of death is as much an art as it is a science." Three days later, however, the judge allowed Anderson to present her evidence in spite of defence attorney Rory Morahan's objections. The lawyer said he was not questioning Anderson's professional training, but suggested her opinion was based on evidence that was "fraught with error, variables and danger." The judge disagreed, saying the existence of variables affected only the weight Anderson's testimony was given, not whether she could give an opinion.

In his closing argument, Morahan said that since three witnesses had seen one of the women after May 3, when his client could prove he was in northern B.C., he could not have committed the murders. Crown attorney Rick Wallensteen argued that the defence witnesses were mistaken.

The jury deliberated for nine hours before concurring with Wallensteen and Anderson and finding Doherty guilty on two counts of first-degree murder. He was sentenced to life in prison.

In 1992, four years and several dozen cases after she saw her first decomposing body, Gail Anderson became Canada's first full-time forensic entomologist. The position is funded jointly by Simon Fraser University and the B.C. Coroners Service. Although her peculiar specialty is beginning to pique the interest of homicide investigators across Canada and will undoubtedly play an increasingly important role in solving murders, the science behind picking bugs out of bodies is overshadowed by the latest newcomer to the forensic field — the esoteric discipline that can allow scientists to identify a perpetrator from a single drop of dried blood.

BIOLOGICAL CALLING CARDS

T HIRTY-FIVE YEARS AGO, when Norm Erickson was just starting his career, he and his fellow analysts in the biology section at the Ontario Centre of Forensic Sciences used to break out the champagne when the bloodstain on a crime exhibit turned out to be type AB, the rarest of the four main blood groups. Most stains were O or A — 47 percent of the province's population had the first, and 40 percent, the latter — and therefore were not particularly meaningful as evidence in a court case. Only 4 percent of the population had type AB, however, making such rare identifications a cause for celebration.

Little did Erickson and his colleagues know back in 1959 that discoveries in molecular biology would, in short order, render such typing extremely crude by comparison. After all, it was just six years earlier that James Watson and Francis Crick described the twin spiral structure of DNA, the molecules of heredity. Few could have predicted that their finding would quickly lead not only to an entire new industry of biotechnology but to the greatest breakthrough in forensic science this century.

By 1970, the advent of a technique called electrophoresis allowed analysts like Erickson to refine their blood typing by distinguishing among the various enzyme components in blood. Biologists welcomed the advance, never dreaming that, in little over a decade, a British geneticist would have devised a way to distinguish virtually everyone in the world, with the exception of identical twins, through the genetic equivalent of fingerprints.

In the early 1980s, Alec Jeffreys of the University of Leicester discovered that certain segments of human deoxyribonucleic acid, or DNA, are identical in every cell nucleus in one body but different from person to person. Furthermore, he found that a print of these sections could be made through a multistep process that uses enzymes to cut the DNA strands into specific pieces and then radioactive genetic probes to bind to and illuminate the identifying regions. At the time, Jeffreys had no idea of his finding's potential in forensic science; his research was aimed at uncovering markers for inherited diseases, which would allow for their earlier detection and treatment. But the significance did not escape him for long.

In December 1985, Jeffreys and two researchers from

Britain's Home Office Forensic Service reported in the journal *Nature* that they had isolated intact DNA from blood and semen stains as old as four years. And they had visually matched these stains to fresh blood and semen samples on the basis of the unique sections of their DNA — non-coding sequences called introns that are interspersed among the coding regions of genes. Not only that, but the scientists said they had solved a common problem facing forensic biologists trying to identify a rapist's blood type: they had found a way to isolate semen from vaginal fluid, which has its own DNA pattern.

In a manner uncharacteristic of scientists, the British researchers enthusiastically began their report, "It is envisaged that DNA fingerprinting will revolutionize forensic biology particularly in regard to the identification of rape suspects." They concluded that by using this simple method, forensic scientists could for the first time positively identify a person, whereas in the past they could only positively exclude someone if testing showed his blood or semen did not match samples linked to the crime.

Barbara Dodd, a professor of blood group serology at London Hospital Medical College, was more cautious in her assessment of the breakthrough in an editorial in the same issue. "Excitement concerning the application of DNA fingerprinting to forensic science has to be tempered by the realization that much assessment remains to be done," she wrote. "If this proceeds satisfactorily, it will be difficult to disagree with the prediction of [Jeffreys and his colleagues]."

The mainstream media picked up the story the same week. In Canada, the *Globe and Mail* quoted Jeffreys as saying the odds of two individuals having precisely the same pattern of these sections of DNA were one in ten billion billion.

Since the world's entire population is only five billion, these were astronomical odds, indeed. Shortly after, an article in *Science News* described the probability of chance association as one in thirty billion. In their original report in *Nature*, the researchers had stated the probability was less than 5×10^{-19} when separate probes are used to illuminate two identifying regions of DNA. They would soon be forced to rethink these figures, but not before the technique was put to its first forensic test.

In the summer of 1986, police in the English Midlands called on Jeffreys for help in a homicide investigation. Two fifteen-year-old girls had been raped and strangled, three years apart, but within one and a half kilometres of each other. A week after the second murder, a seventeen-year-old porter at a local mental hospital confessed to the killing. The police wanted to know from Jeffreys whether the porter was also responsible for the first murder.

After producing DNA profiles on the semen samples recovered from each body, the geneticist came to the conclusion that both girls had, indeed, been murdered by the same man. But the porter was not that man. Convinced that Jeffreys could determine who was, the police asked some four thousand men who lived or worked in the area to donate blood for DNA testing. Many months later, before all the analyses even finished, one of them was overheard bragging in a pub that he had given a sample under the name of his friend, baker Colin Pitchfork, at his request. Police tracked down Pitchfork, who took one look at the new science of genetic testing and pleaded guilty.

Over the next three years, however, the technique was the source of much controversy. The first debate centred around the enormous probability statistics. Critics charged that they were based on the assumption that all people marry randomly and their offspring therefore inherit random genetic traits. In reality, the detractors said, many people marry within their own ethnic groups or even subgroups, which reduces the probability of two people having the same DNA print to maybe one in a hundred thousand. The purists pointed out that all of the statistics being bandied about were based on nothing more than theory; they called for comprehensive population studies to produce the necessary data on which to properly calculate the reliability of the technique.

Even before news of the Midlands case broke, laboratories around the world, including the Ontario Centre of Forensic Sciences, the RCMP's central forensic lab in Ottawa, and the FBI had assigned serologists to investigate the potential of the new tool. The enthusiasm of these government-funded labs was held in check in part by the expensive, labour-intensive nature of the work. Even today, conventional DNA testing on the simplest case takes about six weeks and costs between $600 and $800 in chemicals alone. Beyond the issue of money, the public labs were mindful of the meticulous expertise and depth of experience required not only to do the initial work but to read and interpret the final prints, called autoradiographs, whose black and grey bands resemble a supermarket bar code. The crime labs were also well aware of the damage that could be done if they presented the technique in court before they had done the groundwork — established what happens when DNA degrades or is contaminated by bacteria or the elements, for example, or shown which bodily fluids or tissues best preserve DNA over time.

In 1988, after two years of preliminary research into DNA typing by forensic serologist Gary Shutler, the RCMP intensified its efforts. It began formally collaborating with other Canadian scientists working in the field and with the FBI. And it recruited two young experts in the new field of molecular genetics: John Waye had earned a PhD in medical biophysics from the University of Toronto and then spent two years as a postdoctoral fellow in the university's department of medical genetics; Ron Fourney had a PhD in biochemistry from Memorial University of Newfoundland and had done three years of postdoctoral studies in molecular evolution and the molecular basis of cancer predisposition at the University of Alberta. They were joined the next year by a third specialist, John Bowen, who joined the RCMP in Edmonton as a hair and fibre analyst after obtaining a PhD in biochemistry at the University of Alberta. Together the scientists, assisted by three technologists, began laying the foundation for the official establishment of the force's molecular genetics section.

While the government labs in Canada and the United States were slowly and methodically moving into the business of DNA profiling, a few private labs in the U.S., recognizing the enormous commercial value of the technique, were steaming ahead full-throttle in uncharted and unregulated waters. And therein lay the root of the second debate to rock the legal community's confidence in what may well be the most important forensic tool ever developed: quality assurance — a particularly contentious issue considering that a single test can exhaust all of the available DNA in a crime exhibit.

One of the quickest companies off the mark was

Lifecodes Corporation in New York. By the spring of 1989, when the RCMP and the FBI began accepting requests from law-enforcement agencies for DNA testing, Lifecodes and two other private labs in the U.S. had already been consulted in hundreds of criminal cases. Just a few months earlier, Lifecodes was quoted as saying no court had ever ruled its evidence inadmissible.

In a milestone ruling that summer, Judge Gerald Sheindlin criticized Lifecodes for its sloppy work in the murder case against New York City janitor Joseph Castro. Castro was accused of stabbing to death Vilma Ponce and her two-year-old daughter in their South Bronx apartment in February 1987. One of the crucial pieces of evidence was a small bloodstain found on Castro's watch. Lifecodes tested the stain and reported that it matched Ponce's blood.

In an unprecedented move at the pretrial hearing, a distinguished group of scientists, called in by both the prosecutor and the defence to assess the DNA evidence, got together outside the courtroom and issued a statement challenging Lifecodes' testing. They noted that the autoradiograph bands had been assessed solely by eye, that two of them fell outside the acceptable margin of deviation according to their computer analysis and that there were two extra blurry bands in the watch sample that Lifecodes had discounted as contamination, probably from bacteria. "The data in this case are not scientifically reliable enough to support the assertion that the samples . . . do or do not match," the experts said. "If these data were submitted to a peer-reviewed journal in support of a conclusion, they would not be accepted."

Judge Sheindlin ruled that while DNA typing is "generally acceptable in the scientific community and can produce reliable results," Lifecodes had "failed in several major respects to use the generally accepted scientific techniques and experiments for obtaining reliable results." The results of Lifecodes' testing, he said, would not be admissible.

A furore erupted as observers predicted that the ruling would encourage every American who had been convicted on the basis of DNA evidence to challenge the procedure used to identify them. The debate intensified when one of Castro's defence attorneys, Peter Neufeld, co-wrote an article on forensic science for *Scientific American* in May 1990. His co-author was Neville Colman, director of the Center for Clinical Laboratories at Mount Sinai Medical Center in New York City.

The lengthy and wide-ranging critique began by reminding readers that half a dozen suspected IRA terrorists, who became known as the Birmingham Six, were convicted in England in the mid-1970s of bombing two pubs after a forensic procedure called the Greiss test revealed traces of nitrites on their hands — traces that would be consistent with the recent handling of explosives. The men, who were arrested as they disembarked from a train that had left Birmingham just before the explosions, spent sixteen years in prison before it was discovered that a variety of common substances such as old playing cards and cigarette packages also yield positive results in the Greiss test. It turned out that the men had spent most of their train ride playing cards and smoking cigarettes.

"The Birmingham case raises troubling issues about the application of forensic technology to criminal investigations.

Since the discovery of fingerprinting . . . science has assumed an increasingly powerful role in the execution of justice. Indeed, scientific evidence is often the deciding factor for the judicial resolution of civil and criminal cases." The problem is, Neufeld and Colman said, that most lawyers, judges and jurors are not scientists and cannot properly assess scientific methods and arguments. Their scientific illiteracy is compounded by the fact that judges rarely question the validity of a particular kind of scientific evidence once it has been accepted by another court in an earlier case. "The frequent failure of courts to take a fresh look at the underlying science has been responsible for many a miscarriage of justice."

Zeroing in on DNA testing, the authors then slammed the private labs for their hype: "Promotional literature distributed by Lifecodes asserts that its test 'has the power to identify one individual in the world's population.' Not to be outdone, Cellmark Diagnostics in Germantown, Md. — Lifecodes' main competitor — claims that with its method, 'the chance that any two people will have the same DNA print is one in 30 billion.' Yet, as testimony in the Castro case showed, such claims can be dubious."

In calling for mandatory accreditation of forensic labs and for national standards to be established before a scientific technique can be transferred from the laboratory to the courtroom, Neufeld and Colman charged, "There is more regulation of clinical laboratories that determine whether one has mononucleosis than there is of forensic laboratories able to produce DNA test results that can help send a person to the electric chair."

As the FBI and others in the U.S. scrambled to control the damage to DNA typing's credibility by establishing uniform standards for protocol and quality assurance, Canadian forensic scientists working on the new technique gave thanks that the labs in this country had proceeded so cautiously. "The controversy confirmed that we were wise to go slowly," comments Doug Lucas, director of the Ontario Centre of Forensic Sciences, whose lab was working on its first three cases when the *Scientific American* article was published.

In some corners, the relief had a hint of smugness. "See, the problem in the United States," says Cpl. Bob Stair, an identification specialist at the RCMP's Vancouver lab, "is that every little place has its own little police department. If you're the chief of five policemen in a small town and you have one murder every five years, it is very attractive for you to phone up Lifecodes and say, hey, can you do it? You don't know anything about quality control or anything — you just hand over your money and away you go. We are finding now that there could be all sorts of things that could lead to a false identification if you haven't done your homework. We have had some criticism because we are so slow getting off the ground. But I can tell you when DNA profiling does come on line here, it will be done properly."

The RCMP had actually come on line in Ontario in April 1989 in the case of Paul Joseph McNally. The thirty-two-year-old Ottawa man was charged with breaking into the home of a sixty-eight-year-old woman while she slept and with forcibly confining and brutally raping her. He had been to the house a month earlier to repair the basement floor. The day after the attack, McNally was identified in a police photo lineup and arrested. Married with two children, he steadfastly maintained his innocence and voluntarily provided blood, hair and saliva samples for serology and hair and fibre analyses at the Ottawa lab. When the scientists identified stains on the victim's nightgown and bedspread as semen, the RCMP's DNA experts decided it was time to put their typing procedure, by then three years in the research-and-development stage, to the test.

Seven months after the assault, McNally's case came to court. He pleaded not guilty. On the third day of the trial, a voir dire — a trial within a trial — was held to determine the admissibility of the DNA testing. Judge Keith Flanigan of the District Court of Ottawa-Carleton ruled that the DNA evidence was admissible and in fact was no different than the fingerprint, blood or fibre evidence that had been accepted for years. Molecular geneticist John Waye then explained to the jury how he had used the new technique to match the semen stains in the victim's bedroom to the blood samples provided by McNally.

Since sufficient DNA was extracted from the exhibits, the RCMP was able to produce prints of five separate identifying regions. The information was then digitized and fed into a computer that compared it with population databases and spit out a specific statistic on the chance of another individual having precisely the same pattens. In McNally's case, the odds were one in several billion. After listening to Waye's testimony, McNally suddenly changed his plea and confessed to the crime. He was sentenced to seven years in prison.

"What this test shows," Waye commented afterwards, "is that no matter how normal a person appears or how well he lies, there is a biological test that can be used to find out the truth."

One of the first DNA cases for the Ontario Centre of Forensic Sciences involved the 1990 murder of Elizabeth

Bain, a twenty-three-year-old student who attended the Scarborough campus of the University of Toronto. Bain was a psychology and sociology major who worked part-time with handicapped individuals and enjoyed jogging and playing tennis. She was last seen about 6 p.m. on June 19, sitting on a picnic table on the campus grounds watching a tennis game. Three days later, her silver 1981 Toyota Tercel was found abandoned less than a kilometre from her home. The car was bloodstained but empty.

In the basement of the Ontario centre, analysts from the biology section and others pored over the vehicle. At the same time, police investigators went through Bain's diary looking for clues. They also mounted an infrared scanner, which they had borrowed from the RCMP, onto a helicopter and flew over the woods and parks surrounding the university looking for hot spots that might indicate a decomposing body. Four months later, neither the police nor the hundreds of volunteers who helped search for the young woman had turned up any trace of her.

From the outset, the detectives said later, the prime suspect was Robert Baltovich. The twenty-five-year-old psychology graduate had dated Bain for more than a year and had been questioned several times about her disappearance. Just after dawn on Monday, November 20, 1990, he was arrested at his home in Scarborough and charged with second-degree murder.

When the case came to trial in the spring of 1992, Crown attorney John McMahon theorized that Baltovich had taken Bain into the secluded woods around the campus and killed her because she wanted to break up with him. He then concealed her body and went to the campus recreation centre to establish an alibi. After dark, he returned to the scene, recovered the body, put it in her car and later drove it fifty kilometres north to Lake Scugog, an area he knew from working there as a camp counsellor in his teens.

The case was a rarity in Canada because there was no eye witness to the crime and no body. Two of the almost one hundred witnesses who testified during the six-week trial said they had seen Baltovich near Lake Scugog shortly after Bain's disappearance; one picked him out of a police lineup as the man he had seen driving Bain's car after her disappearance. A third, a jail guard, said the accused told him after his bail hearing that there was no chance Bain's body would ever be found.

In spite of the copious bloodstains in Bain's car, without a sample of the victim's blood, there was nothing to compare the bloodstains with. Baltovich's lawyer argued that there was no evidence that Bain was even dead, much less murdered. However, the DNA evidence suggested otherwise. Biologists at the Ontario Centre of Forensic Sciences had done a sort of reverse paternity test on the bloodstains in the car. When they compared the DNA profile exacted from these with the profiles of samples from Bain's parents, they concluded that the stains could only have come from a female offspring of those parents.

After fifteen hours of deliberation, the jury found Baltovich guilty. In response to his protestations of innocence, Mr. Justice John O'Driscoll remarked, "You are highly intelligent but devoid of a heart." Adding that he had a right to expect justice but no claim to mercy, the judge increased the time before his mandatory life sentence could be appealed to seventeen years from ten.

Six months earlier, in October 1991, DNA profiling was put to its toughest test to date in Canada in the multiple murder trial of forty-three-year-old Allan Legere, a resident of the Miramichi area of eastern New Brunswick. In May 1989, Legere was serving a life sentence at Atlantic Institution in Renous for the beating death of John Glendenning, the sixty-six-year-old owner of a small general store east of Chatham, when he broke away from two guards at a Moncton hospital where he had been taken for treatment of an ear infection. Despite one of the largest manhunts in Canadian history, in which police searched the Miramichi woods on foot with dogs and by air with heat-sensing radar as in the Bain search, Legere remained at large for almost seven months.

Three weeks after his escape, two elderly sisters who operated a small corner store in Chatham were savagely beaten, raped and left to die by a masked man who robbed their store-top home late at night and then torched it. Firefighters found the body of Annie Flam, seventy-five, in the smouldering rubble. Her sister, Nina, sixty-three, survived but was critically injured.

Almost five months later, on October 13, 1989, a nearly identical crime was committed. Two middle-aged sisters, who lived alone in their childhood home not far from the Newcastle wharf, were tortured and raped, and their two-storey wooden house was ransacked and set on fire. This time, though, firefighters found both Donna Daughney, forty-five, and Linda Lou Daughney, forty-one, dead, their faces literally shattered.

A wave of fear overtook the Miramichi region. In the town of Newcastle, Halloween trick-or-treating was cancelled and there was a sudden rise in requests for gun permits by the town's five thousand residents. Some elderly couples took to sleeping in shifts.

On November 15, 1989, the killer struck again. Father James Smith, an elderly Roman Catholic priest in Chatham Head, across the river from Newcastle, was found slashed and beaten to death in his blood-splattered rectory. Residents of the picturesque area, now more panicked than ever, reacted with anger when the media dubbed their region the murder capital of Canada.

Nine days later, Legere was captured by heavily armed Mounties at a police roadblock in Nelson-Miramichi. He had commandeered a tractor-trailer, and another trucker had alerted police on his CB after seeing the rig travelling down a side road not usually used by trucks.

It took a full year for the RCMP's forensic scientists to complete their testing on the many exhibits recovered by police at the three crime scenes; when they did, Legere was charged with all four murders.

No fingerprints were found at the scenes. However, a bloody footprint was found on a church bulletin on the rectory floor and, even more important, semen had been recovered from three of the female victims of Legere's brutal attacks; in the case of the Daughney sisters, the stains, invisible to the naked eye, were illuminated when the bodies were scanned with a laser at the RCMP's forensic laboratory in Halifax.

Billed as New Brunswick's trial of the century, the case was tried in the fall of 1991. As the so-called monster of Miramichi sat chained to the floor and guarded by a small army of police officers, Robert Kennedy, an RCMP expert in the physical matching of human feet and footwear, and his counterpart from the FBI, testified that it was highly probable that Legere wore a pair of boots that left the bloody print on the church bulletin. The jury had already heard that the nicks and marks found on the sole of one of a pair of Greb Kodiaks, found near the train station in Bathurst the day after the priest's murder, matched the print left at the scene. Having established that the boots were at the scene, Kennedy sought to prove to the jury that Legere was in the boots. He showed a ten-minute video of the procedures he had followed in making detailed plaster moulds of Legere's feet and the boots' insoles. It ended with an image of the feet fitting perfectly into the boots. Not only were the contours a match, Kennedy said, but the tip of a nail that protruded up through the heel of the left boot aligned exactly with an odd reddish-brown mark on the accused's left heel.

Crown attorney Jack Walsh — who himself became a virtual expert in DNA typing during the year he spent preparing for the trial — called all three founding scientists of the RCMP's molecular genetics section at the Ottawa central forensic laboratory. John Waye, who by then had left the force to assume a faculty position at Hamilton's McMaster University and to run the molecular diagnostic laboratory at Chedoke-McMaster Medical Centre, began by giving all assembled a lesson in the basics of DNA testing. Asked how inbreeding might affect the results of DNA testing, Waye said a Washington-based study on a South American tribe in which everyone descended from one king and his three queens showed that despite inbreeding over many generations, DNA testing could uniquely identify everyone. The key, he said, was to illuminate more than one identifying region of each person's DNA through two or more probes.

Next, the Crown called John Bowen to explain specifically the results of DNA testing done on semen recovered from Nina Flam and the bodies of Linda and Donna Daughney. With the lights in the courtroom dimmed, Bowen flashed slides onto a large screen of DNA profiles produced from hair and blood samples taken from Legere and of prints from the semen samples, pointing out the matches. In all, sixteen tests had linked Legere to the three women, Bowen said. He explained the statistical probability that the semen could have come from another Caucasian male. In the case of Donna, there was one chance in 7,400; for Nina, one in 5.2 million; and for Linda, one in 310 million.

Kenneth Kidd of Yale University, a pioneer in DNA printing, testified next that he not only agreed with Bowen's results, he thought Bowen had been too conservative in discarding some DNA matches as not close enough.

Finally, Ron Fourney, as head of the RCMP's molecular genetics section, took the stand to address the issue of quality control in the lab. Questioning him about the long hours that he and his colleagues work, Legere's lawyer, Weldon Furlotte, remarked, "Tired people make mistakes." Without missing a beat, Fourney replied, "Inexperienced people make mistakes."

The jury also heard from two more DNA experts: George Carmody, an authority in population genetics at Ottawa's Carleton University, and William Shields, a zoology professor at New York State University in Syracuse and author of *Inbreeding and the Evolution of Sex*. Both agreed with the RCMP's results, although Shields, who was called by

Furlotte, opined that the probability statistics quoted in the case of Linda Daughney were perhaps closer to one in eleven million.

Carmody suggested that the defence attorney was "preoccupied with the difference between odds of one in five million and one in 300 million. . . . In the end it doesn't really matter. When the odds are that high, both are a very rare occurrence."

Ultimately, Furlotte argued that the science of DNA typing was too new, too untested, to be relied upon to convict a man of such serious charges. However, Mr. Justice David Dickson, in his five-hour charge to the jury, commented that "the use of DNA testing is in its infancy in this country but that doesn't mean it's any less reliable as a forensic tool. . . . I think it's fair to assume that DNA typing is here to stay."

The jurors deliberated for thirteen hours over two days before finding Legere guilty of four counts of first-degree murder; he was sentenced to life in prison without the possibility of parole for twenty-five years. In January 1993, the New Brunswick Court of Appeal granted Legere leave to appeal his convictions on the basis of the admissibility of DNA fingerprinting; the panel of three judges denied ten other grounds. Five months later, during the actual two-day appeal, Weldon Furlotte again questioned the statistical probability that the DNA extracted from semen found at the crime scenes matched the DNA in Legere's hair; Jack Walsh pointed out that even William Shields, the expert called by the defence at Legere's 1991 trial, put the probability that the DNA could have come from someone else at one in eleven million. The Court of Appeal judges reserved decision on the case and gave no indication of when their ruling would be released.

By spring of 1994, the RCMP had scientists working on DNA cases at three of its forensic labs — Ottawa, Edmonton and Halifax — and had just finished training others to take on such cases in Vancouver and Winnipeg. By then, experts at the first three labs had presented evidence in court in sixty cases, firmly establishing DNA typing as one of the most powerful weapons in the forensic laboratories' arsenal.

Research and development is now under way in a technique called polymerase chain reaction, or PCR. It allows scientists to take minute bits of DNA, say the amount found in a single speck of blood, and clone it until there is a large enough sample to work with. Those studies, in conjunction with the current scientific push to identify every component of the human genetic code, may one day lead to a whole new generation of DNA testing: deriving a physical description of a perpetrator from a single hair or other biological "calling card" left at a crime scene. PCR will also likely reduce both the cost and analysis time required by the procedure.

DNA research is already being used in increasingly varied ways. In British Columbia, a man murdered a woman and transported her body to a dumpster, which he doused with gasoline and set afire, incinerating her remains. When DNA extracted from the pulp of an embedded wisdom tooth was shown to match DNA in the blood in the killer's car trunk, he was convicted. In Spain, forensic odontologist David Sweet is currently researching the theory that DNA could be obtained from the sloughed-off epithelial cells in the saliva often found on bite marks.

Research being conducted by Gail Anderson and others also suggests that DNA typing might save time for forensic entomologists, allowing them to identify the species of insects from larvae without having to raise them to maturity in the lab.

As the potential for this molecular tool increases, it seems likely that the debate on whether police in Canada should be allowed to demand a blood or hair sample for DNA testing from an accused person — as is the case in some American states — is also bound to grow. Critics of the civil rights argument point out that although the Canadian Charter of Rights prohibits the police from even seizing, for example, a cigarette butt that a murder suspect has smoked during questioning, it is against the law for someone suspected of drunk driving to refuse to provide the police with a breath or blood sample. Indeed, the more sophisticated and esoteric all forensic techniques become, the more complicated the politics surrounding them.

SCIENCE ON THE STAND

O VER THE PAST CENTURY and a half, ever since James Marsh figured out how to detect the presence of arsenic in the body and Marie Lafarge was convicted of murder as a result, science has assumed an increasingly important role in the administration of justice. In fact, as juries demand more and more hard evidence for convictions, physical evidence has become far more powerful than such personal evidence as eye-witness accounts. There is a consensus that whereas people may convincingly lie, forensic technology is always factual and impartial.

As forensic science becomes increasingly multidisciplinary and high-tech, however, the potential for the wealth of additional information it generates to be misunderstood looms ever larger. Most police officers, lawyers, judges and juries do not have scientific backgrounds. This means not only that they have to rely on the varying abilities of scientific experts to explain their findings but also that they are ill equipped to assess the weight of the scientific testimony. The problem is compounded because the same evidence can sometimes be interpreted in various ways.

As Alexander Lacassagne, one of the pioneers of modern forensic pathology, remarked a century ago in Lyons, France: "One must know how to doubt." The doctor was commenting on the sometimes surprising inconsistencies he had encountered in attempting to determine the time of death according to standard rules. Since then, medical knowledge has exploded and forensic pathology has become a sophisticated specialty. Still, the task of deciphering the cause, manner and circumstances of an unnatural death is as much an art as it is a science. As a result, forensic pathologists are frequently called upon to interpret unique evidence and give opinions. This can be dangerous territory for anyone inclined to conjecture.

Over the course of his twenty-five-year career, James Ferris can recall several instances in which he was aghast at the evidence a colleague offered in court. One case, which still stands out, occurred in Toronto in the mid-1970s. Garbagemen had discovered inside a sack in a trash bin the torso of a woman, her head, arms and legs sawed off. Ferris had just arrived in Canada after serving as assistant state pathologist in Northern Ireland and then consultant pathologist to the Home Office for the North East of England. As

Ontario's new deputy provincial pathologist, he conducted the autopsy.

The same week, a man told city police that his housekeeper had disappeared. The last time he talked to her, she had confided that she had been giving money to a male acquaintance to forward to her family in India and had just found out it was not getting there. The employer offered to send the money himself in the future. The woman left the house and was never seen again. In due course, the torso was identified as that of the housekeeper, the embezzler was arrested, and Ferris was called to court to testify about the cause of death.

The victim appeared to have died of an airway obstruction, Ferris told the court, but he said he could not identify the mechanism of obstruction. The Crown was dissatisfied and called in another forensic pathologist, who reviewed the medical evidence and came to a different conclusion.

"Much to my disgust," recalls Ferris, "he stood up in court and said that death was due to strangulation. I didn't see how he could say that since there was no neck available."

Sensing a loophole he could exploit, the accused immediately turned to his lawyer. "Will I be set free if I can prove I did not strangle the woman?" he whispered.

"Of course," his attorney replied.

"Fine. I'll tell you where the head is."

Much flurry ensued, the trial was adjourned, and the investigators set off to recover the head, which the accused had buried in a marsh nine months previously. For some strange reason, he had coated it with the oily tar used on the outside walls of basements to prevent them from leaking. Then, he placed it in a tote bag before interring it in

the bog. Consequently, the head was remarkably well preserved.

By examining the head, Ferris was able to confirm that
the woman was not strangled. She had been beaten around
the face and her jaw had been broken in two places. Back in
court, the accused admitted striking the woman but said he
had not intended to kill her; he testified that she passed out
and shortly afterwards stopped breathing. His story was consistent with the medical evidence. After she lost consciousness, her tongue, as a result of her bilateral jaw fracture, had
fallen back, blocking her air passage. The defendant was
convicted of manslaughter.

The case is a classic illustration, says Ferris, of the errors
that can occur when reconstructions are not solidly based in
fact. In this case, the problem was that the expert apparently
allowed his ego to interfere with his opinion. But sometimes,
it is a matter of fundamentally different approaches to scientific evidence — scientists failing to understand the expecta-
tions of the legal system, and police, lawyers and courts not
comprehending the nature and limitations of forensic evidence.

What Ferris wishes every non-scientist connected with
the judiciary would accept is that even in the most exact
areas of forensic science, no conclusion can be considered
absolute. Proof is measured in degrees of probability based on
the knowledge, training and experience of the scientist. And,
in all cases, an opinion is only as valuable as the evidence on
which it is based. "The key for forensic pathologists is to recognize their own fallibility, to be able to say, 'I don't know,'
or 'I'm wrong,' or, hardest of all, 'My opinion is based on the
information that was available to me and if additional infor-

mation comes out, I reserve the right to change my opinion.'"

He knows from experience how unpopular such admissions can be. He was once criticized by a judge for changing his opinion. "I said, 'I was given incomplete information.' And he had the audacity to say to me in court, 'Dr. Ferris, do you mean you were prepared to give an opinion without all the information?' How do I know what all the information is? I felt he was not being reasonable."

As forensic science becomes increasingly esoteric, Ferris says it is more important than ever to restrict opinion witnesses to their areas of proven expertise, regardless of their degrees, titles or status. But that is only one area that must be approached with caution if the court is not to be misled. Careful attention must also be paid to issues of co-ordination and communication. Without a scientific overseer, he says, an investigation can suffer from tunnel vision, especially when community pressure is combined with excessive zeal on the part of the police or Crown attorneys.

On January 31, 1969, a bitterly cold Saturday in Saskatchewan, David Milgaard, a sixteen-year-old high-school dropout living in Langenburg, set out from Regina at one in the morning to visit an acquaintance, Albert Cadrain, in Saskatoon. With him were two teenaged friends, Ronald Wilson and Nichol John. The three planned to see Cadrain and then go on to Alberta. They travelled through the night in Wilson's old Pontiac and arrived in Saskatoon about 6 a.m. The temperature was nearly forty degrees below zero and an icy fog limited visibility. The teenagers drove around in the dark looking for Cadrain's house in the neighbourhood of Pleasant Hill.

At about six-thirty, they pulled up beside a woman walking along a sidewalk and Milgaard asked her for directions. When she said she couldn't help, Wilson drove up the block a little way and tried to make a U-turn; the car got stuck in the snow. Milgaard and Wilson set out in opposite directions in search of help. Within about fifteen minutes, both had returned. Two male passersby, who were never identified, helped to free their car and the three youths drove away. Their vehicle got stuck once again and had to be towed before they finally reached Cadrain's house at about nine o'clock.

Half an hour earlier, in a back alley close to where their vehicle was first stuck, a young schoolgirl was taking a short-cut when she came across the partially clad body of Gail Miller, a young nurse's aide. Miller had been scheduled to begin work at City Hospital at seven-thirty that morning. She was apparently on her way to catch a bus when she was raped and stabbed repeatedly. Four months later, Milgaard was charged with her murder.

The trial began in January. T. D. R. Caldwell represented the Crown; Cal Tallis was appointed by the government to act for Milgaard. Caldwell called to the stand the three young people who had spent the weekend with Milgaard. Nichol John and Ronald Wilson testified that they had seen Milgaard with a small paring knife on the way to Saskatoon. And when Milgaard arrived back at the car after going for help, they said, he was breathing heavily, as though he had been running, and told them, "I fixed her." Later, Wilson and Cadrain said, they saw what they thought was blood on Milgaard's pants. At four-thirty that afternoon, the four had set out for Alberta. When it was Milgaard's turn to drive, he was speeding in spite of the icy roads. At one point, they added, John found a compact in the glove compartment, and when she asked who it belonged to, Milgaard threw it out the window without saying a word. Cadrain said that when he returned home to Saskatoon, he heard about the murder, became suspicious of Milgaard and went to the police.

Another acquaintance of Milgaard's, Craig Melnyk, told the court that he was with Milgaard and three other youths in a motel room four months later when Gail Miller's murder was mentioned on the television news. He said Milgaard was high on drugs at the time; when someone asked him whether he had killed Miller, he began hitting a pillow as though he was stabbing it.

In addition to the testimony of Milgaard's friends, the Crown introduced physical evidence that Caldwell said implicated Milgaard. Harry E. Emson, a forensic pathologist from the University of Saskatchewan, told the court that there were fifteen stab wounds in Miller's body, many of which were superficial. Two, though, penetrated the chest cavity and the right lung, and the resulting loss of blood was the cause of death. A small amount of reddish fluid removed from her vagina at autopsy was later found to contain sperm. There was no evidence of forced sex, Emson said, but that did not mean she had not been raped; if the sexual assault occurred when she was unconscious or immediately after she died, her body would have been relaxed.

When Miller was found, her nurse's uniform and her underclothing had been pulled down but her arms had been reinserted into her coat; Emson said there was no indication of whether that happened before or after death. There were cuts in her coat, corresponding to her stab wounds, he said, but none in her dress.

The police testified that on the day of the murder they found, buried in the snow near the victim's body, a three-and-a-half-inch knife blade with the handle broken off and, around the corner, Miller's cardigan and one of her boots. Four days later, they turned up two frozen lumps of a yellowish substance where her body had lain. Her purse was discovered in a nearby garbage can. The handle of the knife was turned in by a neighbourhood boy who found it in his back yard.

A pivotal aspect of the Crown's case — put forward nearly two decades before the advent of DNA testing — was based on Milgaard's blood type. In 80 percent of the population, all of the body's fluids contain antigens that identify a person's blood type. The court was told that the sperm removed from the victim's vagina was not tested for the presence of antigens and was later discarded. However, tests were performed on the frozen yellowish lumps found at the scene. An analyst testified that one of the samples contained sperm with type A antigens. A later experiment also revealed traces of blood.

Milgaard had type A blood. But there was a glitch. A test of his saliva showed he was a non-secretor; if so, his semen would not contain type A antigens. To explain the contradiction, the Crown introduced evidence that it was possible Milgaard had suffered an injury to his penis or urethra and, as a result, his blood had contaminated his semen.

The jury deliberated for eleven hours before finding Milgaard guilty of non-capital murder. He was sentenced by Judge A. H. Bence to life in prison.

In 1988, forensic pathologist James Ferris was asked by Milgaard's new lawyer, David Asper, to review the evidence presented at the 1970 murder trial. By this time, T.D.R. Caldwell was a federal prosecutor in Saskatoon; Cal Tallis was a judge with the Saskatchewan Court of Appeal; and Joe Penkala, one of the original investigating officers, was Saskatoon's chief of police. Just as he had with the dingo-baby case in Australia, Ferris questioned both the validity of some of the samples and the overall reconstruction of the crime. He was particularly critical of the serology evidence presented at the trial. Not only did it fail to link Milgaard with the murder of Gail Miller, Ferris concluded, but it "could reasonably be expected to exclude him from being the perpetrator."

The theory that Milgaard's blood contaminated his semen is unlikely, Ferris said, especially since there was no evidence that Milgaard was suffering from any bleeding injury. He added that neither he nor several forensic colleagues he had consulted on the matter knew of a single case in which semen was contaminated by the assailant's blood.

Considering that the frozen lumps were recovered several days after the murder, Ferris said he was surprised they were even considered admissible evidence. There was evidence that the scene had been extensively trampled by police officers and medical examiners and that snow was shovelled to one side in the search for the weapon. Consequently, mixing of evidence would be almost bound to happen.

Ferris questioned whether Milgaard even had enough time to commit the crime. The autopsy results suggest that Miller would have lost consciousness and died slowly. "It is possible, in fact, that she could have survived for at least fifteen minutes following the injuries." Furthermore, he said, the cuts to her garments indicated that her coat was taken off, her underclothing pulled down, and her coat put back on before she was stabbed. "It also suggests that the circumstances of the rape/murder were complex, probably prolonged, and in my opinion, incapable of having occurred within the time frame suggested by the evidence at the trial."

Considering the case from a standpoint of plain common sense, Ferris said he was doubtful that the crime as described could take place outdoors in minus-forty-degree weather. Although noting that there was no clear evidence on the matter, he said, "The general circumstances of the scene would tend to indicate to me that the offence may have taken place elsewhere and that the body had been dumped."

Ferris's report was submitted by David Asper to the federal Justice Department with a request for a new trial. When, sixteen months later, the department still had not responded, Asper asked another forensic pathologist, Peter Markesteyn, the chief medical examiner for the province of Manitoba, to conduct a second independent review.

In his eight-page brief, submitted in June 1990, Markestyn said he could reach no conclusion about whether Milgaard had sufficient time to commit the crime. However, he shared Ferris's concerns about the integrity and continuity of the samples of alleged semen recovered from the scene four days after the murder. And he went one step further. "Yellowish stains in snowbanks most commonly find their origin not in human ejaculates, but in urine, most commonly of canine origin."

Markesteyn noted that unused semen in dogs is not

reabsorbed but rather is secreted in their urine; dogs urinate over each other's urine and semen to establish territory. As well, dogs have antigens that serologically cross-react with human A antigen. Finally, he said, human semen does not freeze into a yellowish stain at minus forty degrees; it is white and difficult to spot in snow without special techniques such as ultraviolet light. The Winnipeg doctor questioned the method used to detect the presence of blood in the frozen specimens: "This in all probability was the Hemastix test and, if so, would have been used contrary to the manufacturer's instructions, which specifically limit the use to a screening test for blood in urine."

In conclusion, Markesteyn agreed with Ferris that the physical evidence failed to link Milgaard to the crime. "In my opinion, the serological evidence presented at the trial was on very shaky scientific grounds to a degree that it may very well have been erroneous. I do not know what effect, if any, this evidence had. . . . Unless another trial were held, we will never know if another jury, properly instructed on the scientific merits of these forensic tests, would draw another inference."

By the time Markesteyn's report was released, the case was already the subject of national media attention. According to Asper, Justice officials had tracked down a witness, never called at the original trial, who signed an affidavit refuting Craig Melnyk's account of Milgaard's actions in the motel room. The officials had also received a statement from another person who said he gave the same information to the Saskatoon police department in 1980, implicating a convicted rapist in Gail Miller's murder; at the time she was killed, the man was living in a basement apartment in the same house as Cadrain. John Harvard, the member of Parliament for Winnipeg who raised the issue in the House of Commons and at a House justice committee meeting, told reporters that the Justice Department was dragging its feet as a result of pride. "People's reputations are at stake. If they did submit it to the courts, it would be a tacit admission of failure by some fairly high-profile people."

A year and a half later, in November 1991, the Justice Department asked the Supreme Court of Canada to review the case to determine whether Milgaard's conviction constituted a miscarriage of justice and, if so, what remedial action, if any, was advisable. During the thirteen days of hearings, held over the first four months of 1992, Ronald Wilson recanted his 1970 testimony, Nichol John said she remembered little of the events of that day, and several witnesses gave vastly different versions of the alleged stabbing re-enactment in the motel. The court was told that Albert Cadrain was a police informant and had been paid $2,000 for helping to secure Milgaard's conviction. Finally, evidence was presented that showed that the timing, location and pattern of Miller's murder was consistent with four other sexual assaults in Saskatoon to which another man had confessed and was serving time.

In its judgement, the Supreme Court ruled that it was "not satisfied either beyond a reasonable doubt or on a preponderance of the evidence that the accused was innocent. However . . . his continued conviction would be a miscarriage of justice if a jury could not consider the fresh evidence. However, if a new trial were directed and the accused were found guilty, the court would recommend that the Crown consider granting him a conditional pardon." In other words, perhaps to avoid the issue of compensation, the Supreme Court was not saying he was guilty or innocent. After serving twenty-two years in prison for a crime he has steadfastly maintained he did not commit, Milgaard was released. Seventeen months later, in September 1993, the Saskatchewan Court of Queen's Bench ruled that Milgaard can sue Crown prosecutors and the police officers involved in his 1970 murder conviction for compensation.

In 1986, Ferris and Laurel Gray were involved in an informal review of another Canadian case in which a convicted murderer has tenaciously protested his innocence. Again, the forensic pathologists believe that the scientific evidence does not support the reconstruction of the crime.

Marian Ruddick, a fifty-three-year-old Ottawa housewife, was found face-down in about eighteen centimetres of water in the bathtub of her suburban bungalow just after 10:30 a.m. on November 16, 1976. Her husband, Frederick, manager of a life insurance company, told the police he had left home more than an hour earlier to try to stave off their eviction from the house. Unbeknownst to his wife, Ruddick was deeply in debt and several months in arrears in rent; he said he did not tell her about his financial problems because she had previously suffered a nervous breakdown and he wanted to protect her from further stress.

When Frederick returned home after failing to raise enough money to forestall the eviction, he found bailiffs inside his house trying to open the bathroom door. He got a meat skewer from the kitchen and forced the lock. When the door swung open, they saw Marian lying in the tub; the water was lukewarm and tinted blue by a large quantity of bath oil. When it was determined that she had no pulse, Ruddick acted excited, according to an assistant with the sheriff's office, who said, "If it had been my wife, I would have been in a state of shock."

An ambulance was called and Marian was taken to Ottawa Civic Hospital, where her heartbeat was restored through electroshock and cardiopulmonary resuscitation. However, she never regained consciousness and died that night. An autopsy the next morning showed that there was no water in her lungs, indicating that she probably had not drowned, but the post-mortem failed to uncover the cause of death. Her body was cremated.

An insurance company executive said that at Marian's wake Frederick was extremely emotional and obviously in great distress. As the police investigated her death, however, they became increasingly suspicious of Ruddick. He owed $42,000, including $8,000 to Revenue Canada for unpaid taxes. There were two life insurance policies in his wife's name, one taken out in 1966 and the other in 1970, which together would pay $31,000 in the event that she died accidentally.

The day Marian died, two detectives who attended the scene observed that the shower curtain was ripped at the top seam under the first three hooks. They also uncovered a one-and-a-half-metre extension cord under some clothes in a hamper in the bathroom, although they noted that the nearest electrical outlet was roughly two and a half metres from the bathtub. They found a flimsy plastic bag on the floor in the master bedroom, which was later tested for fingerprints with no results. They also noted that Marian's housecoat was on top of her nightgown on her bed, the opposite of what would have been expected if she had undressed in her bed-room before having a bath.

The Ruddicks' twenty-two-year-old daughter told inves-tigators that her mother usually bathed in the evening, undressed in the bathroom and wore a bathing cap in the tub. She had not been wearing the cap when she was found.

The physician in charge of the emergency department when Marian arrived at the hospital said there were no bruises on her head, neck, chest or back; however, there were superficial abrasions on her knees, shins, ankles, stom-ach and right arm. The pathologist who performed the inconclusive autopsy told the police that although he could not rule out death from natural causes, he considered the possibility slight.

What really aroused the suspicions of the investigating officers, they said later, was that Ruddick lied when they asked him whether he had ever had an extramarital affair during his thirty-three years of marriage. "Absolutely not," he told them. It turned out, though, that not only had he had a seven-year affair with his secretary, and paid for her furnished apartment, he also had sex occasionally with a twenty-five-year-old former girlfriend of his son. The last occasion had been the night of his wife's funeral.

Ferris was working in Toronto when the initial investi-gation was conducted and was asked by the police for his opinion of the medical evidence. He was not at all ambiva-lent: there is no proof that Marian Ruddick was murdered, he told them. Ferris says the detectives consulted another forensic pathologist, who took the opposite tack: he said there was no evidence that the woman had died of natural causes. In February 1977, three months after his wife's death, Ruddick was charged with murder.

At his trial, the second pathologist told an Ontario Supreme Curt jury that Ruddick could have killed his wife by one of three means: by suffocating her with a soft plastic bag; by wet electrocution with low voltage; or by applying pressure to the vagal nerves in her neck, which would cause reflex cardiac arrest. None of these methods would leave any marks on the body. The pathologist added that the circumstances were just "too tidy" for an accidental death; in his opinion, it would have been almost impossible for her to have fallen in a small bathtub without injuring her head or splashing water on the floor.

A professor from the University of Florida College of Medicine, who was recognized as an authority on drowning, told the court that autopsies of drowning victims show that 90 percent have water in their lungs; therefore, there was only a 10 percent chance that Marian Ruddick had drowned.

Tests conducted at the Ontario Centre of Forensic Sciences showed a trace of the tranquillizer Librium in Marian Ruddick's blood. However, a Toronto specialist in internal medicine testified that the amount was too small to cause intoxication. He added that he did not believe that her heart had stopped beating because of a heart attack, but when asked by Ruddick's lawyer what he thought had caused her heart failure, he said he had no theory.

At one point during the six-week trial, a full-scale replica of the Ruddicks' bathroom, complete with toilet, bathtub and clothes hamper, was erected on one side of the courtroom. A mechanical engineer from the Ontario Centre of

Forensic Sciences conducted a series of tests for the jury using three sets of shower curtains and hooks, custom-made by a Montreal company to replicate those in the Ruddicks' home. Three times, a fifty-two-kilogram woman, approximately Marian Ruddick's size, climbed into the tub, held a portion of the curtain and simulated falling; only when she grabbed the curtain with both hands did it tear. The implication was that if she had accidentally fallen, she probably would not have clutched the curtain with both hands and it would not have ripped.

The Crown prosecutor postulated that Ruddick murdered his wife because he could not face a confrontation with her over his financial problems, which, in turn, would expose his long-term affair with his secretary. After killing her in one of the three ways suggested by the pathologist, he then put her body into the tub and tore the bathroom curtain to make it look as though she had fallen.

In his charge to the jury at the conclusion of twenty-three days of testimony, Mr. Justice John O'Driscoll seemed to support the leap from pathological liar to pathological killer. Although he reiterated the defence lawyer's point that the jury members were not there to pass judgement on the accused's morals, he also called Ruddick a "chronic liar" and said that if he was found innocent, then mounds of injustice had been heaped upon him by his arrest, but if found guilty, "then he is a cunning, crafty killer who almost pulled off the perfect crime."

Ruddick's lawyer called no witnesses on his behalf. In his three-hour closing address, he said simply that since no cause of death had been determined, the Crown had failed to prove its case. The prosecutor had taken a "shotgun approach" against his client, he said, which required the jury to engage in guesswork.

The jury disagreed. Ruddick was convicted of first-degree murder and sentenced to life imprisonment. When asked by the judge if he had anything to say to the court, he replied: "No, just to reiterate what I have said all along: I am not guilty of that charge."

In 1984, eight years after Ruddick was sent to prison, the CBC television program *the fifth estate* began investigating the case. It asked several forensic experts across North America, including James Ferris and Laurel Gray, to review the medical evidence presented in court. Without exception, all were critical of the lack of information contained in the autopsy report. Gray said bluntly: "There was a castle of cards built on this report. All of the expert witnesses in the world can't come to any real conclusion on the basis of this amount of information."

Because the autopsy report contained absolutely no indication of foul play, Gray added, it was more likely that Marian Ruddick died of natural causes than that she was murdered. Ferris agreed, noting that generally, if a death is unnatural, "the evidence of the injury or the unnatural event is not difficult to detect. We do know, however, that there are very many natural causes of death, perhaps involving the electrical system of the heart, that can cause sudden death and leave nothing to find."

Charles Petty, a forensic pathologist in Dallas, Texas, said it appeared to him as though a lack of co-ordination and communication had hindered the investigation. It seemed that the doctor performing the autopsy had very little information about the case at the time of the post-mortem.

Similarly, he theorized, the scientists in the forensic laboratory who performed the blood and urine analyses probably were detached from the detectives and the pathologist. When three separate entities are working in isolation on the same case, he said, their conclusions usually range from not useful to erroneous.

As Ferris looks back on the case today, he remains certain that justice was not done. "Now Ruddick may have killed his wife. But our job is to allow proof beyond a reasonable doubt and not to be party to reconstructions which are not based in fact. We are convinced that there was insufficient evidence to say there was a murder."

The outcome of the reviews of this case has been quite different from those of David Milgaard's. Frederick Ruddick has exhausted the judicial appeal process and, unless he receives a federal pardon, will remain in prison, serving a life sentence for murder.

Although the defence attorney at Ruddick's trial did not challenge the scientific evidence introduced by the Crown, perhaps as a result of scientific illiteracy, frequently lawyers go out of their way to find experts who will present opposing opinions and then leave it to the jury to sort out which scientist is right. If they cannot find a dissenting scientist, they often pull out all the stops to discredit not only the expert's findings but his or her personal credibility.

It is one of the ironies of working as a forensic scientist that the diversity of your caseload leads, on the one hand, to increased job satisfaction and, on the other, to a need for research in areas with no precedents. And as many have experienced first-hand, citing the results of original research in court is like waving a red flag in front of a defence counsel, especially when the lawyer is someone like Edward Greenspan.

Glenn Carroll, a civilian scientist at the RCMP's central forensic laboratory in Ottawa, was asked in 1988 by the Ontario Centre of Forensic Sciences, as an outside expert, to do the glass fracture analysis in conjunction with a high-profile case in which two police officers were charged after a black teenager was shot west of Toronto.

Wade Lawson, the seventeen-year-old driver of a stolen sedan, was struck in the back of the head by the last of six bullets fired at the car. He died the next day in hospital. The officers said they fired at the rear tires after Lawson ignored their order to stop and tried to run them down. The final bullet blew out most of the rear window, which was tinted tempered glass — a safety glass about which little had been published. Carroll was asked to determine the last bullet's point of impact, which would indicate where the gun had been pointed.

When the scientist arrived at the OPP garage on Harbour Street in Toronto, where the car was being held, it appeared to him, from the glass remaining in the frame, that there was a series of radial fractures that pointed back to one location. His first plan of action, when he arrived back at his lab, would be to project straight lines back from the fractures to see where they converged; he would use red thread, which would photograph well.

With the help of an OPP officer, he removed the entire back window, encased it first in foam and then in plywood, and taped it securely. They also removed the fuzzy shelf liner under the back window, which was covered with pulverized glass fragments, and, taking care to keep it horizontal, packaged it in similar fashion. Finally, in case it would be necessary to reconstruct the window, they picked up every one of the thousands of tiny cubes of broken glass. The evidence was then transported to the RCMP lab in an OPP van.

Carroll subsequently determined that the bullet entered the window about forty centimetres from the frame on the passenger's side and the same distance up from the bottom of the frame. After he had submitted his report, the Crown attorney called in a firearms expert from Phoenix, Arizona, to conduct experiments on a replacement window in the same car. Lucien Haag shone a laser along the sights of a police revolver to determine the trajectory between Carroll's estimated point of entry and the driver's seat and then pulled the trigger. "Lo and behold," says Carroll, "the deflection was less than an inch." In other words, Haag's experiment supported Carroll's own findings.

With almost twenty years' experience as a forensic analyst, which included hundreds of court appearances, Carroll realized that his evidence was "more common sense than cutting-edge technology," but he thought his testimony would be straightforward. He was wrong. After the preliminary hearing and before the trial, he conducted some more tests at the RCMP's firing range with six rear windows made from tempered glass, which he purchased at a junk yard. "I was fairly confident," he explains, "but I didn't want to be vulnerable at the trial." Little did he know that these experiments would lead to even more criticism.

Carroll spent nine days on the stand, testifying at the preliminary hearing, the trial and a voir dire to determine the admissibility of evidence. "I have never gone through anything that gruelling," he says. In the mock trials that forensic science laboratories hold to determine whether a recruit, who has successfully completed every other aspect of his or her training, has what it takes to withstand cross-examination in court, Carroll says he had never been that belligerent when it was his turn to play the defence attorney. "Now, I have no qualms."

During the voir dire at the preliminary hearing, Edward Greenspan, a well-known criminal lawyer defending one of the police officers, slowly warmed up to the task of destroying the scientist's admissibility as an expert witness in the case.

"Do you have any certificate in glass fracture analysis?"

Carroll explained that he was certified by the RCMP as a specialist in hair and fibre examinations, which includes glass fracture analysis.

"How many hours have you spent on glass fracture analysis?"

In excess of one hundred hours, Carroll replied.

"How much of that time was spent on glass fracture analysis of bullets going through windows of cars?"

Approximately half that time, Carroll said.

"How many cases then have you done where you did not go buy glass to make an experiment . . .?"

Two, Carroll said.

The next day, Greenspan was more aggressive. At one point early on, Provincial Court Judge J. Draper was moved to remind the defence lawyer that "a person who knows a great deal about glass may never have dealt with yellow tinted glass with stripes on it."

Taking a different tack, Greenspan zeroed in on the fact

that the stolen car had been moved by flatbed trailer from the original scene to the OPP garage. During the trip, photographs showed, some cubes of glass fell away from the window.

After interrupting Carroll as he was trying to address the issue, Greenspan finally said, "You wanted to get out what you feel, right, so why don't you get your feelings right out."

"I wanted to complete my answer to your previous question, Mr. Greenspan. That was, the loss of additional glass did not, certainly did not, change the fractures that are present in the pieces still remaining within the frame of the glass."

"How do you know they didn't move . . . which would be central to the question of you having the gall to say forty up and forty over?"

Carroll was, in the end, qualified by the court as an expert witness at the preliminary hearing. After the voir dire, he testified that the spray pattern of pulverized glass on the shelf liner under the back window supported his conclusion that the bullet had entered the window about a third of the way over and halfway up on the passenger's side.

Greenspan returned again to the fact that the vehicle had been moved. "When you got to the OPP garage, you say the shelf liner was removed with the glass fragments situated in much the same location as they had fallen. You can't know that, I suggest to you. You can't know that at all. You take a car, fit it up on a tow. Do you have any idea where it [the car] went?"

"No."

"Fine. So I take it that's not a statement you could vouch for, right?"

"I would have to concede that, yes."

"Okay. Thank you."

"However, by virtue of the fuzzy nature of the shelf liner
—"

"Why don't you just concede it. It would make me feel
so good. But you won't, so go ahead. However, by the very
nature of the shelf liner, by the very fuzzy nature of the shelf
liner, this pile of glass never moved, right?"

"Some of the fragments I don't feel moved substantially."

"What are you, a fuzzy liner expert too?"

A year later, when the case went to trial, Greenspan
asked Carroll why he had taken on the case, was it his only
chance at fifteen minutes in the sun? He also called Carroll's
procedures unscientific and said that the testing he had conducted at the firing range was, in the current age of computers and lasers, "horse and buggy science," rigged to uphold
his original conclusion.

The police officers were acquitted.

Aside from assailing Carroll's credibility, Greenspan's
central argument was that there was little published literature in the field. "He insisted that he get every literature ref-
erence I cited," recalls Carroll. "We'd break for the day and
I'd go to the photocopier with his student and we'd photo-
copy them. The next morning, I'd have them thrown back at
me on the stand.

"The trick is not to lose your cool. It's like trying to fight
someone with one hand tied behind your back, because you
can only respond to what they ask you."

Understandably, many forensic scientists dread the
adversarial nature of court proceedings, but James Ferris and
Larry Cheevers are two who enjoy the challenge. "Be under

no illusions," says Cheevers, "court is theatre. They call Ferris and myself top guns because we put on a good show." The forensic dentist, who took up boxing at university while he had a broken leg in a cast and went on to win the championship four years in a row, relishes the sport of a court appearance. "It's is not unlike a shootout at the OK Corral," he says. "You only have to lose one battle and your credibility is destroyed.

"You've always got to be prepared for the unexpected question that you know is going to come up. Over the past twenty years, I have been astounded at the agility of some of the questions that have come from the defence. They can be quite sticky and unless you are prepared for it, they can make you look stupid."

Computerized information networks are making it more difficult than ever to testify as an expert. "What we are increasingly confronted with is computers that will spit out every legal precedent and every case where bite marks have been involved." There have always been mavericks writing opinions contrary to what is accepted in science, but now large legal firms have the resources to find these obscure papers. "Quite often a lawyer will come in and start quoting from an article that you have no idea about. He says, 'Well, Dr. Cheevers, do you agree with this?' And I say, 'That certainly is strange. That certainly is contrary to anything I've ever seen.' And you ask where the article came from. He says, 'From Botswanaland.'"

Cheevers tells of one case in which an American forensic dentist was asked if he was familiar with a certain textbook. When he answered yes, the defence lawyer said no such book existed. "That was his swan song."

The only option for an expert who is confronted with a paper or book he is not aware of is to admit it and ask for a copy. "If you don't do that and you start arguing with the lawyer on the basis of the statement he has made, not knowing anything about it, bang, there goes your whole case. The jury is looking at you thinking, he looked so competent five minutes ago and everything he said sounded so true. But all of a sudden he is arguing about a silly statement. There are so many tricks to the trade of the defence lawyers of which you have to be aware."

Cheevers says that having "Dr." in front of their names gives Ferris and him some measure of automatic credibility on the witness stand. As does their Irish accent: "It adds greatly to the vocal variety. It is astounding how few people realize that communication is 55 percent visual, 35 percent vocal and 10 percent verbal. From the moment you walk into court, your dress and manner are all part of your evidence. I have always had large visual aids — a picture is worth much more than a thousand words. If possible, I have the jury handle and manipulate my evidence."

Cheevers says that he and Ferris frequently use analogies to explain complex theories to jury members. "There is no point in talking about huge analytical quantum theories of statistical evaluations. You are wasting your time. You just tell them a simple story like a parable and they understand."

The final exit is also critical for any expert, he says. "Gather your papers, rise, bow to the judge, look at the witnesses and the jury and leave in an unhurried and dignified manner."

In routine cases, forensic scientists are not always called to court personally to testify; rather, the reports of their findings are introduced as evidence. Even here there can be communication problems stemming from the precise language that scientists must use. "I've had police officers call me up on hit-and-runs," says an analyst at the Ontario Centre of Forensic Sciences, "and say, 'You said in your report that the paint on the exhibit is consistent with the paint from the suspect's vehicle. With all the expensive equipment that you scientists have up there, you mean you can't say anything more than I can say?' What they fail to understand, the analyst says, is that to a scientist the expression "is consistent with" is stronger than "could have come from." They also do not realize that the scientist must back up his statement with information available in his laboratory's databases. And while his computer can spit out hard numbers on how common a certain refractive index is in glass, for example, it does not have such definitive statistics on paint.

Sometimes a single word can cause a problem. The analyst recalls one instance in which a colleague used the word *volatile* in a report. "All he meant was that the liquid to which he was referring evaporated quickly. The person reading the report thought the word meant flammable. As a consequence, there was a considerable misunderstanding."

What all of these problems — from experts going beyond the facts to non-scientists failing to understand either the facts or their importance — underline to James Ferris is the need for a scientific overseer with a broad perspective and base of experience. He or she would be appointed at the onset of a complex investigation to ensure that no avenue of exploration is overlooked, that the efforts of the police and scientists are integrated and, ultimately, that the lawyers and the court are provided with an overview of the scientific merits of the case. If the case involves particularly specialized analyses, such as DNA testing, two or more scientific advisors from different fields might need to be appointed.

Although it might appear that scientists are less impartial if they work with the police, the two groups have different mandates; the scientists' success is not measured by whether an accused person is found guilty. Brian Dalrymple, the civilian analyst employed by the OPP in its Toronto laboratory, puts it this way: "I was supposed to get the maximum evidence out of an exhibit. I am excited when I find a fingerprint, excited when I can make an identification. But if I cared whether this evidence resulted in a conviction, I'd have a drinking problem. If I can get the maximum evidence and introduce it in court with assurance and integrity, then I'm a happy camper."

That forensic scientists can testify for the Crown on one case and for the defence on the next, and be aggressively challenged by the opposite side in each, also speaks to their impartiality.

The reality is — as the forensic pathologists who reviewed the cases of Milgaard and Ruddick in Canada and the Chamberlains in Australia found — when the key players on the scientific side of a complex investigation work in isolation, without adequate communication with the police and Crown attorneys and without a scientific overseer, justice is not served.

If, on the other hand, a scientific overseer was appointed at the onset to ensure that the appropriate examinations and analyses were conducted at the right time by the most qualified person, and that all of the findings were co-ordinated and properly communicated, the result is more likely to be an accurate reconstruction of a crime.

Implementing such a system would cost money, and may not be welcomed by the traditionally cash-strapped forensic laboratories and the coroner's services who pay for the services of outside forensic science experts, but it would undoubtedly strengthen the multidisciplinary team approach to crime solving that has been so successful in British Columbia.

The wealth of additional information that can increasingly be generated by the growing number of disciplines within forensic science has the potential to ensure, as never before, that the guilty are convicted and the innocent go free. If this burgeoning body of scientific knowledge is underused, or misused, in the future, society as a whole will lose out.

INDEX

Age: estimates based on teeth, 89; estimates based on bones, 128

Alcohol: abnormally high readings in blood, 112–13, 115–16; acute high doses , 115; as a murder weapon, 116–17

American Academy of Forensic Sciences, 134

Anderson, Frank, 6, 8

Anderson, Gail, 145–54, 173–74

Anthropologists. *See* Forensic anthropologists

Anthropometry, 27

Archaeological techniques, 129–30, 134–135, 138, 144

Arkell, Kevin, 131–33, 137–38

Arsenic, 7–10, 14–15, 17–19, 21, 23–26, 37

Arsine gas, 7, 24

Asper, David, 183–85

Aspiration pneumonia, 115

Autopsies, 6, 9, 79, 96–98, 106–8, 119

Autoradiographs, 159, 161

Bailey, F. Lee, 66–67

Bain, Elizabeth, 165–67

Baltovich, Robert, 166–67

Bastien, Bart, 73–83, 107–8, 112–13, 148

B.C. Coroners Service, 74, 95, 154

Beaton, Alexander, 8

Belli, Melvin, 17

Bence, Judge A.H., 182

Bertillon, Alphonse, 27–28

Bertillonage, 28

Bezeredi, Tibor, 112

Bio-Systematics Research Institute, 145

Birmingham Six, 162

Bite marks, 76, 79–88, 173

Blood: alcohol readings, 112–13, 115–17; antigens, 182, 185; blood-stain-pattern analysis, 65–71; elec-trophoresis, 156; groups, discovery of, 28; groups, percentages in Ontario,

155; lividity, 39, 114; under laser or Luma-Lite, 64

Bones: identification techniques, 126–8; retrieving skeletal remains, 130, 134–6, 138

Borden, John, 141, 143–46

Botanical examinations, 144

Bouck, Justice John, 118

Bowen, John, 160, 171

Boyle, Frank, 86

British Home Office, 47, 157

Buckner, Vanessa, 113–18

Bullets, 39–40

Bundy, Ted, 79, 85

Burns, Mary, 40

Cameron, James, 99

Canada: computer program for den-tal files, 91–92; dental impressions from accused, 82; obtaining DNA samples, 174

Canadian Charter of Rights, 174

Canadian Police College, 129

Canadian Police Information Centre, 91

Canadian Society of Forensic Science, 91

Canadian Society of Forensic Science Journal, 139

Carleton University, 67, 71

Carlisle, Sheila, 134–35

Carmody, George, 171–72

Carroll, Glenn, 194–98

Castellani, Esther and René, 1–21, 24

Castro, Joseph, 161–62

CBC: *the fifth estate*, 192

Cellmark Diagnostics, 163

Chamberlain, Lindy and Michael, 98–103, 202

Cheevers, Larry, 73–93, 104–05, 107–08, 123–24, 199–200

Child abuse, 84

Churchman, James, 33

Cirrhosis, 115

Clark, Lisa, 131–38
Colburn, Dennis, 152
Colman, Neville, 162–63
Comeau, Gary, 144–46
Coroners, 74, 93, 106
Cranbrook air disaster, 77–78
Crick, Francis, 156
Criminal Investigation, 29
Crofts, Henry, 26
A Cry in the Dark, 101
Crime laboratories: budgetary constraints, 36, 40, 41, 203; caseloads, 40–41; DNA profiling, 159–60, 164–65, 167, 170–71; history of, 23, 29–36; sections, 41–42; shared expertise, 46–50
Crime-scene investigations: botanists, 144; blood-stain pattern analysis, 65–71; forensic anthropologists, 126, 130, 134–36, 138–39; forensic entomologists, 139,143–45, 148–49; forensic pathologists, 97–98, 106, 113–114, 134–135, 144; identification officers, 51–52, 56, 63–65

Dalrymple, Brian, 57–63, 202
Daughney, Donna and Linda Lou, 168–69, 171–72
Death, determining the time, 114, 141–43, 149, 153, 176
Decomposition of bodies, 129, 141–44, 147–51
Dentists. *See* Forensic dentists
Deoxyribonucleic acid. *See* DNA
Derôme, Wilfrid, 29
Dickson, Mr. Justice David, 172
Direction des Expertises Judiciares, 40
DNA profiling, 56, 156–60, 173–74, 202; Bain case, 165–67; Castro case, New York, 161–62; Legere case, 168–72; McNally case, 164–65; quality assurance, 160, 164; sample from accused, 174
Dodd, Barbara, 157
Doherty, James Andrew, 153–54
Dorion, Robert, 81
Doyle, Sir Arthur Conan, 28–29
Draper, Judge J., 196
Drowning, 190
Drugs, evidence at autopsy, 117
Duff, Jim, 59–61

Electron microscopy, 36
Electrophoresis, 156
Electrostatic detection equipment, 42
Elmira College, New York, 67
Emson, Harry E., 181
Entomologists. *See* Forensic entomologists
Erickson, Norm, 1, 12–14, 17–18, 21–22, 43, 50, 59, 155
Exhibits, packaging and processing of, 56, 135, 152

Facial reconstruction, 129
Faulds, Henry, 57, 63
Federal Bureau of Investigation (FBI), 29, 46–47, 92, 159–61, 163
Felstein, Harley, 108–09, 112–13
Ferris, James, 95–98, 101–104, 105, 106, 109, 112–13, 119–21, 124, 137, 144, 176–79, 183–85, 187, 189, 192, 193, 198–202
Ferry, Judge William, 112
Fibre evidence, 44–47
Fingerprints, 26–28, 33, 56–64
Fisher's method, 10
Firearms identification, 39–41
Fisher, Annie and Nina, 168–69, 171
Flam, Annie and Nina, 168–69, 171
Flanigan, Judge Keith, 165
Flies, 142–43, 145, 147
Fluorescence, 59–61, 63–64
Fontaine, Rosario, 29
Footprints, 169–170
Forensic anthropologists: indentification methods, 126–28; retrieval of skeletal remains, 129, 130, 134–36, 138
Forensic dentists: computer program for dental files, 91–92; dental identification methods, 89–90; history of forensic odontology, 88–90; transillumination of bite marks, 81–82, 84–85
Forensic entomologists: estimating time of death, 141–43, 149, 153–54; collecting evidence, 152
Forensic odontologists. *See* Forensic dentists
Forensic pathologists: autopsy process, 119–20; estimating time of death, 114; role in review cases, 98
Forensic science: definition of, 26; budgetary constraints, 35–36, 40–41, 92, 203; role in the administration of justice, 162–63, 175–79, 201–202; scientific illiteracy, 120–121, 163, 193, 201–202
Forensic scientists: first formally recognized, 26; impartiality, 121, 202; scientific overseer, 179, 201–203; testifying in court, 17–19, 104, 124, 176–79, 193–202
Fourney, Ron, 160, 171
Frankish, Edgar R., 29
Furlotte, Weldon, 171–72

Gas chromatographs, 36
Gaudette, Barry, 46–47
Genetic fingerprinting, *see* DNA profiling

Georgia Crime Laboratory, 46
Gibbons, Velma, 113–118
Glass fracture analysis, 194–198
Glendenning, John, 168
Globe and Mail, 157
Globe Terminal Transportation
Services, 109
Graham, Bob, 87
Gray, Laurel, 104–110, 112–119, 148, 187, 192
Greenspan, Edward, 194, 196–98
Greiss test, 162
Gross, Hans, 29
Gutzeit test, 8

Haag, Lucien, 195
Hair, arsenic poisoning, 9, 10, 12–15, 18, 37
Hall, Charles Francis, 37
Handwriting experts, 42
Harker, Stacie, 86–87
Harmon, Thomas, 9–10
Harper, Lynne, 43
Harry, Vera, 113–18
Harvard, John, 186
Herschel, William, 26, 57
High-tech instruments for crime solving, 36
Hit-and-run accidents, 42
Holmes, Sherlock, 28–29, 55
Hoover, J. Edgar, 29
Hutchinson, Justice Ralph, 153–54

Inbreeding and the Evolution of Sex, 171
Insects, attacks on human remains, 142–43, 149, 150
Iodine-silver plate, 59
Identification officers, 51–52, 55–56, 63–66
Identification techniques: arsenic, 23–26; bloodstain-pattern analysis, 65–71; blood typing, 28, 155–56; dentists, 88–91; DNA profiling, 156–74; fingerprints, 26–27, 56–64; firearms, 39–40; physical measurements, 27–28; skeletal remains, 126–29

Jeffreys, Alec, 156–58
Joe, Sheila, 118
John, Nicol, 179–81, 186
Jones, David, 118
Jones, James Patrick, 86–88
Jordan, Gilbert Paul, 111–13, 116–19
Justice Department: Milgaard case, 184–86
Justice system: forensic scientists testifying in court, 17–19, 104, 124, 176–79, 193–202; Lawson case, 193–97; Milgaard case, 179–86; role

of forensic science, 162–63, 175–79, 200–203; Ruddick case, 184–92; scientific illiteracy, 163, 193, 200–202

Kennedy, Robert, 169–72
Kidd, Kenneth, 171
King, Sarah and Dr. William Henry, 26
Kirk, Paul, 67
Krazy Glue, 63

Lacassagne, Alexandre, 39, 176
Lafarge, Marie and Charles, 24–25
Landsteiner, Karl, 28
Laser examination: fingerprints, 60–64
Lawson, Wade, 193
Legere, Alan, 168–72
LeRoy, Herb, 65–71
Lett, Stephen, 33
Lifecodes Corporation, 161–62, 163
Lividity, 39,114
Locard, Edmond, 27, 29, 56
Loomis, Chauncey, 37
Lucas, Doug, ix–x, 38–39, 40, 42–43, 164
Luma-Lite, 63–64

Macdonald, Sir John A., 37, 38–39
MacDonnell, Herbert, 67
Mackoff, A.A., 18–20
Maggots, 107, 142, 145, 147, 149, 151, 152
Mallow, John, 33, 34
Markesteyn, Peter, 184–85
Marsh, James, 24–26
Mason-Rooke, Andrew, 36
Mass spectrometers, 36, 41
May, Lucas S., 30
McAuley, Frank, 49
McGee, Thomas D'Arcy, 37–39
McGill, Frances, 34
McGillvray, Dr. Donald, 37
McInnes, Guy, 131–33
McMahon, John, 166
McNally, Paul Joseph, 164–65
Megnin, J.P., 143
Melnyk, Craig, 181, 185
Mengele, Josef, 84
Menzel, Roland, 59–61
Milgaard, David, 179–86
Miller, Gail, 180–83
Mites, 142
Morahan, Rory, 153–54
Morgue, 106–08
Morris, Dael, 151
Moscovich, Bernard, 3–8, 18

Nature, 57, 157, 158
Nerve tissues: arsenic, 9, 18, 19
Neufeld, Peter, 162–63
Neutron activation analysis, 12–14, 37

Newbury, Louisa, 49–50
Nielsen, Finn, 44
Ninhydrin, 57, 63
Noronic disaster, 90–91

O'Driscoll, Mr. Justice John, 167, 191
Olson, Clifford, 95
O'Neill, Edward, 38, 40
Ontario: coroners, 74
Ontario Centre of Forensic Sciences, 12, 29, 38, 40, 41, 43, 48, 67–68; DNA testing, 159, 164, 165, 167
Ontario Provincial Police, 48; forensic laboratory, 58, 62
Orfila, Mathieu, 25

Pathologists. *See* Forensic pathologists
Peel, Dr. H.W., 41
Petty, Charles, 192
Philp, Michael, 44–45
Physical measurements, 27–28
Pitchfork, Colin, 158
Police: crime laboratories, 30, 34–36; entomologists and, 150–51; fingerprint identification system, 64; sample for DNA testing, 173–74; tension between scientists and, 119–21
Polymerase chain reaction (PCR), 173
Powers, Maurice, 29–33, 34
Primeau, Lex Arthur, 153
Pringle, Kerry, 153
Psychological assessments, 55

Quebec: coroners, 74; North America's first forensic laboratory, 29

Revere, Paul, 88
Rideout, Eldon, 8, 10, 11, 13, 17
Rigor mortis, 114
Robinson, "Robbie," 32
Royal Canadian Mounted Police (RCMP): computer program for dental files, 91–92; crime laboratories, 29–36, 40, 41, 42, 46, 47; DNA profiling, 159, 160, 161, 164–65, 170–172; identification officers, 51–52, 55, 56
Ruddick, Marian and Frederick, 187–93

Saliva, 80, 173, 182
Sarcophagidae, 142
Science News, 158
Scientific American, 162
Scientific illiteracy, 120–21, 163, 193, 201–202
Sellers, Ruth, 108
Semen: DNA testing, 157, 182–84
Serology, 28
Shade, Edna, 113–18

Sharpe, Noble, 34, 35
Shendlin, Judge Gerald, 161–62
Sheppard, Sam and Marilyn, 67
Shields, William, 171
Shutler, Gary, 160
Simon Fraser University, 126, 134, 141, 154
Skeletal remains, retrieval of, 129, 130, 134–36, 138
Skinner, Mark, 127, 129, 134–39, 141
Skull, 54–55, 127–29, 136–37
Slattery, Timothy, 38
Smith, H. Ward, 33–34
Smith, Father James, 169
Stair, Bob, 146, 164
Strangulation, 79
Strongman, Brian, 51–55, 123–30, 134–37
Supreme Court of Canada: Milgaard case, 186
Sweet, David, 78, 80, 84, 173
Syed, Akbar, 141, 143–45

Tallis, Cal, 180, 183
Tammie, Aaron, 82–83, 85
Taylor, Harold, 18–19
Technology: high-tech instruments for crime solving, 36
Teeth: bite marks, 76, 79–88, 173; dental identification methods, 88–91; pink-teeth phenomenon, 77–78
Temperatures: life span of insects, 149
Thomas, Patricia, 113, 119
Time of death, 39, 114, 141–43, 149, 153, 176
Toxicology, 24, 26, 36–37, 41
Transillumination, 81–85
Truscott, Steven, 43

Ultraviolet light, 63
United States: dental impressions from accused, 82; DNA testing in private labs, 160–163

Video equipment, 85
Vincent, Verda, 29

Walsh, Jack, 170, 172
Warren, Gen. Joseph, 88
Watkin, John, 63
Watson, Don, 137
Watson, James, 156
Waye, John, 160, 165, 170
Whelan, Patrick James, 38–39
Williams, Wayne Bertram, 46–47
Wilson, Ronald, 179–80, 186
Wilson, Rosemary, 117
Woodward, Kimberley Jean and Gene, 48–50